Ron Carter

Harbour Books

Claremont, California

Published by:
Harbour Books
147 Armstrong
Clarmeont, CA 91711

Library of Congress Cataloging-in-Publication Data

Carter, Ron, 1932-
　　Me & the Geezer / by Ronald G. Carter.
　　　　p.　cm.
　　　　Summary: His first summer in California looks bleak for Joe Russell, as he endures his father's lectures and finds him self stuck playing Pony league baseball with a group of misfits that is a far cry from the championship team he played with last year.
　　　ISBN 0-9643672-2-X (alk. paper)
　　　[1. Baseball--Fiction. 2. Fathers and sons--Fiction.] I. Title.
PZ7.C24785Me 1996
[Fic]--dc20   95-51021
                                                                           CIP
                                                                           AC

paperback ISBN: 0-964-3672-2-x

Text design and production: Graphic Relations
Cover illustration: Cathy Morrison, Big Chief Graphics
Printing: Publishers Press, Salt Lake City, Utah

10 9 8 7 6 5 4 3 2

To Joe

INTRODUCTION

Athletics have always been a part of life in our family. My wife and I have five sons and three daughters, all of whom have been active in school and summer sports. We once estimated that all combined, we have watched our children participate in at least four hundred eighty competitive basketball, volleyball and baseball games, through seventeen seasons, junior and senior high school. With each game, the kids gave us something to treasure in our hearts.

However, it was when our youngest child, Joseph, played his Pony League baseball season that we suddenly realized unique things were happening. Joe had an unbelievable gift in his pitching arm. The previous year he had pitched his Utah little league team to the State Championship, then won the first game at the Northwest Division playoffs in Aurora Colorado.

Then we moved to a small town in Southern California, where no one had ever heard of his pitching arm, or his talent for baseball. The coach for Joe's team was out of town on business the day they divided up the players and assigned them. As a result, Joe found himself on a team named the Reds, that had every reason to lose every game that summer. It was a mix of all races, all sizes, all social backgrounds, and very little baseball talent. They had one practice before they played their first game, and Joe came home that afternoon absolutely devastated, muttering, "That bunch of misfit nobodies is going nowhere."

Joe's arm won the first game, and the coach won the second one. From that point on, something hilarious, or weird, or unheard of happened every time they played. More unbelievable was the fact the team kept winning, to the utter amazement of everyone who knew anything about baseball.

We watched tall, gangly Bernie, the rich African American kid, stop in the midst of a crucial play to check the trademark on the baseball, because he wanted to see what company made it. We winced when Stone, our eighty pound third baseman speared a rocket line drive that turned him around twice and nearly fused his mitt to his hand. We trembled when Chin, from Taiwan, got in the face of an umpire, shrieking Chinese epithets that the umpire could not understand. And we shouted ourselves hoarse when Mendoza, our two hundred twenty pound Hispanic who stood five feet four inches tall, got his only hit of the season, and caught his only fly ball, in the championship game. We nearly fell off the bleachers when Harry, playing on an opposing team, pulled a groin muscle, which resulted in his father dumping twenty pounds of ice in his pants and sitting him on the bench while the ice melted and puddled around his feet.

There was more, much more, and when the season ended with the Reds finally coming together as a solid team, winning the City championship, we knew we had to commit it to writing. I talked with the coaches, and the players, and we checked the season's score book to be sure we had the team names and the scores right.

This account of that Pony League baseball season tells the story. We loved every minute of it. We hope you do too.

Ron Carter

1

THE NEW KID TRIES OUT

"TELL THEM ABOUT YOUR arm." The Geezer signals for a left turn and slows the Chevy.

"Warm up good, and don't throw before you're ready. Throw before you're warm, your season could be over right now."

He turns left off Baseline and starts down this road with a big concrete storm drain beside it, behind a high chain link fence, and ahead I can see the front of the grade school where they got tryouts.

"And," the Geezer continues, "tell them about Utah. Be sure that arm's warm before you go out there on the mound."

He turns left again, into the parking lot beside the school, and down through a bunch of trees I see the grass and the backstop, and the baseball diamond. There's a lot of kids in baseball uniforms hanging around, watching, and some are walking to their bicycles, and there's a pitching machine on the pitcher's mound. A big pear shaped guy in a beat up old baseball uniform, with bristly straight hair sticking out from beneath his baseball cap is running the machine, and the hair's partly gray, so he's got to be old.

1

The Geezer shoves the Chevy into park and shuts off the engine, and looks over at me.

"Ready?"

I'm looking out the windshield at the tryouts and I shake my head. "Not yet."

He settles back, irritated. "What's wrong? You shaky?"

I keep looking out the windshield.

"Come on," he says finally. "They're about finished."

"They're not throwing," I say. "They're only batting."

"What?," he says in surprise, and he leans over the steering wheel and studies the tryouts for a minute.

"What's wrong with those guys," he says. "You're supposed to throw and field at tryouts, not just bat."

I shrug. "They're only batting."

The Geezer looks disgusted. "Well, okay, we'll go out there and bat. Keep your head down, and keep your eye on the ball, and . . ."

"I'm going alone," I say as I turn my face to him. "I'll go do this alone."

"No," he says, "I better . ."

I cut him off. "I'll go alone."

I don't know the words to say how sick I am of getting this stuff from the Geezer. Always, always, he's telling me what to do, and when, and where, and what expression to have on my face, and what to wear, and what to say, and he's always talking to people like I'm stupid and can't talk to them myself. Never never never has he ever said I did anything right, and always, no matter what I do, he shows me and tells me where I could have done it better.

I wanted to ride my bike and do this all myself, but he said no he'd drive me, and now he wants to go out there with me like I'm a trained robot or something, to say what he tells me to say, and do what he tells me to do.

Deep anger starts churning and I get the sick stomach that always comes when he does this stuff, and the worst part is, I've thought about it a lot, but I can't find a way out.

See, the Geezer is fifty six years old. I'm the youngest of eight kids, and I was born when mom and the Geezer were about forty two. I got four older brothers and three sisters who are all away at school, or married, and the older boys were all good athletes. That was all great while the Geezer was younger, but fifty six? He's lost it. All he does is lecture and criticize, lecture and criticize, lecture and criticize.

He wants me to tell them about Utah. We just moved from a little tiny, dinky town in Utah, and last summer I pitched my little league team to the Utah championship, and then we went to the Northwest Regional Playoffs in Aurora, Colorado. I pitched the first game and we beat a team from California. The rule was no one could pitch two consecutive games, so I couldn't pitch the second one and we lost. But I pitched the third one and we won, and we made it to the semifinals, and I couldn't pitch that game and we lost.

That second game, when I couldn't pitch, our coach played me in center field. The other team got a runner around to third base, and the next guy hits this monster shot to me in center. Their guy on third tagged up to run home after I caught it, and it looked like he could make it at a trot. I mean, there I was, this tall, skinny kid out there in center field, two hundred fifty feet from home plate, and what thirteen year old kid is going to throw a ball from center field to home plate in time to nail a runner coming in from third?

I caught the ball with my back against the chain link, and took my two steps and fired, and I don't think that ball got twenty feet off the ground. It cut a straight line to our catcher, Todd, and he took it at the knees while the guy coming in from third was still ten feet off the plate. The guy saw it, and it shook him so bad he stopped stone still and his mouth fell open, and Todd walked over and tagged him out.

So now the Geezer wants me to go down there and tell the guy running this tryout, "Hey, I got a big league pitching arm, and I pitched my Utah little league team to the state championship, and I fire like a rifle from center field."

I mean, when you sign up for tryouts and you've paid your fifty bucks, who needs to go out there and give commercials? Walk out there and do whatever they tell you, and don't make any excuses and don't give any commercials. Being the new kid in town don't make no difference. Just go do it.

"All right," the Geezer says, "you want me to stay here in the car. Is that where we are?"

I don't look, but I know he has that expression that says I'm a dumb know-it-all kid that don't really know anything.

"Yeah," I say, and jerk the door handle on the Chevy, and I step out into the warm, mid-morning southern California sunshine. I walk through the shade of the trees out into the bright light, over towards the backstop, and I stand around there with my head sort of slouched down and my hands in my hip pockets, waiting for someone to call my name or say something. While I'm waiting I begin to notice how these guys are dressed and what they're doing, and it takes about five seconds to figure out what's going on.

There's one bunch standing out behind third base, and they're wearing white shorts and big, long sleeved shirts with broad stripes, and two hundred dollar Reeboks. Behind the backstop, where a leaky drinking fountain has made a mud hole, there's some other guys standing around, and they're wearing plain old white T-shirts, and old shorts, and beat up cleats or tennis shoes. The Reeboks bunch is talking among themselves, and pointing around, and acting like the tennis shoes bunch are on some other planet. The tennis shoes bunch are quiet and sort of pretending they don't notice the Reeboks bunch, and it doesn't take much to see we got a snobby rich bunch putting down the others.

"Joe Russell."

The old guy on the mound is looking at a clipboard, and he calls my name again. "Joe Russell. Is Russell here?"

"Here," I say, and walk out towards him while I adjust my mitt on my left hand.

"You paid?" He runs a finger down the list on the clipboard.

"Yeah, fifty bucks." I answer.

"Oh, yeah, here it is. You're paid. Okay. Grab a bat. You're the last one." He points towards home plate.

"Do we throw and field and run, too," I ask.

"No, just bat. I can tell from that."

In a pig's eye! I pull off my mitt and look for a thirty two ounce Easton aluminum bat, but they haven't got one so I settle for a thirty ouncer, and I walk back to the plate and I know, I just absolutely know that I'm going to mess up.

See, I've had this problem since I was little. I can take a base-ball and I can pick out a spot like a catcher's mitt, and I can throw full bore and hit it dead center nearly every time. But batting? For some reason I can not explain, I can't make a bat meet a baseball smack on the button. I pop out and I ground out, and I strike out, and once in a while, by accident, I get a hit. My batting average since I was eight years old is about .270, which is low. Sometimes better, sometimes worse, but just hanging around at about .270, and I just hate it.

I kick the dirt until my feet feel right, and I cock the bat over my right shoulder and the old guy out there drops another ball into the induction hole and the spinning wheels catch it and throw it right down the middle, belt high.

I swing and I might just as well have been waving at the seag-ulls.

Fourteen more times, and I finally get a little tiny piece of the last one, enough to knock it foul down the third base line.

The old guy out there makes some marks on his clipboard, and looks at me and says, "Okay. That's it. You'll get a call."

I pick up my mitt and turn to him one more time. "We don't throw?"

He looks at me like I'm dimwitted and says, "No, just bat. I can tell from that."

I nod and walk around behind the backstop and watch my feet to avoid the mud hole by the drinking fountain, and I start through the crowd with the tennis shoes, when one of them says, "You new?"

"Yeah."

"What position?"

"Pitch. And field."

"Oh."

"Who's the guy out there with the machine?," I ask.

"Shellins."

"He know everybody?"

"Yeah, he coaches one of the teams. Been running Pony League here since George Washington invented baseball. Knows every kid in town."

"Yeah," I say sarcastially, "except the new ones."

I walk on through the trees, back to the Chevy, where the

Geezer's waiting in the car with the windows all down. Somehow he knows. He starts the car engine and backs out, waiting for something from me. I slump down and keep my eyes on my feet and don't say a thing.

"Hit any?," he asks, kind of light and airy. I keep my head down but I know he has that dumb look on his face like he thinks he's popped a funny, and I feel my face go red.

"Did he tell you which team you'll be on?" The Geezer's breezy about the whole thing, like nothing has happened. He does that sort of thing to me. I've told him a dozen times about it but he just says things like, "If you're going to be in sports, you got to learn to handle the ups and downs. That's what it's all about."

See, besides being old, the Geezer has another problem. My four older brothers were all state class basketball players, and my three sisters all played basketball or volleyball, and one of them was girl athlete of the year at high school, and another one was All State Academic basetkball player. So the Geezer and Mom have seen about four hundred basketball and volley-ball games with the older kids, and he thinks he's the resident American authority on kids in athletics. Old guys get like that.

"Someone's supposed to call," I tell him.

"Okay," he says and shrugs like, big deal, "we'll wait for the call."

He turns back onto Baseline and starts humming one of those dumb little songs that he sometimes hums or sings quiet-ly, where he makes up his own words that he thinks are funny. I don't know where he gets them - some of them had to come from the dark ages.   It was one of these old poems of his that got him tagged with the nickname Geezer. One day the whole family was in the car and the Geezer was driving, and he start-ed to recite this poem like it had some great message or some-thing.

"There was an Old Geezer who had a wooden leg,
He had no tobacco, no tobacco could he beg."

I looked out the car window and closed my eyes. Where does he get this junk?

"Said the first Old Geezer, will you give me a chew,
Said the second Old Geezer, I'll be darned if I do."

It hurt to listen to the stuff.

"If you'll save up your money and you'll save up your rocks,
You'll always have tobacco in your old tobacco box."

He stopped talking and looked at the family like he's delivered the original Ten Commandments. I couldn't believe the look on his face.

"Get anything out of that?" He waited for someone to say something about finding a great secret for guiding our lives.

"Yeah," I said finally. "A nickname for you."

I thought it would make him mad, but it didn't. He looked disappointed for a few minutes and didn't recite any more of his gems of wisdom or ancient history for a while, but then began to hum again.

From that day on he's been the Geezer.

He turns left on Florence Street, and I don't even think about looking out the window at the yards we're passing. Our new town has laws, and everybody's yard is filled with flowers and shrubs and green grass, and palm trees, and the streets are lined with trees, some of them old giants with bark that hangs in shreds and drops off, and they look really old and stately. We drive around nearly every day because we've never seen a town so neat and well kept. Mom just shakes her head and oh's and ah's all the time.

And at the south end of town we've got these five colleges, and the campus is like out of a picture book. You stand on a corner and watch, and you can see one of every kind of person in the world.

Down by the colleges is The Village. It's the old town, and they painted the old, small shops neat colors, and put cobblestones at the intersections, and it's real special to go down to the village and see the shops and watch the people.

But on this drive back from the tryouts to home, I don't even look out the window at all this neat stuff.

The Geezer parks the car on the driveway and gets out. I sit there slouched over while my mind struggles with what I can expect from that lousy, rotten tryout where all I did was fan the air with a bat.

My mind toys with newspaper headlines: "JOE RUSSELL SETS NEW BATTING RECORD FOR CONSECUTIVE

7

MISSES. The tall new kid in town tried out for the baseball team and set a new International Record. Fourteen misses before he finally touched the ball."

People will point when I walk down the street, and high school kids will smirk. I'll be the only kid in school this fall that no one wants on a team. I'm looking at the big time rottenest, worst summer of my life, all because of my crummy batting eye.

When it gets so hot in the car I start to sweat I finally pull the handle and swing my legs out onto the concrete driveway. I just as well go inside and face Mom and get the pain over with.

2

MOM IS AN OLYMPIC CLASS worrier. If there's nothing to worry about it worries her crazy, and she worries most about us kids. Something bad happens to one of us kids, like the lousy tryout I just had, she hurts worse than we do. I didn't know a human being could take all the worrying she does.

Like in Utah two weeks before I pitched the game that won the Utah State Championship last summer.

What happened was, we moved to a new home two blocks from the old one, which put us one block over the city line that separated Mapleville from Springton. I played for Mapleville before the move, but after the move I lived in Springton. Both towns together don't have three thousand people - just two little dinky towns and no one cares which side of the line you're on.

That is, until you start talking little league state baseball championship.

Anyway, before we moved, Mom called the little league president, a baldheaded guy named Owen Patrick who couldn't find home plate without a map, and she says, "Will it be all right if Joe still plays on his old team in Mapleville?"

"Yes," Patrick says, "he should finish the season on the team

9

he started with."

Great. No sweat.

Then we beat the Panthers, who were in third place, and that meant we had to play the second place team, and you guessed it. Springton.

Man, did things get hot.

It started four days before the game, when some parents from Springton protested. They called up Patrick and they said, "Since the Mapleville pitcher now lives in Springton, he can't play on a Mapleville team any more."

Patrick lives in Springton.

Mom yells, "Dirty politics!," and she paces and stews and gets ready for the shootout.

Two days before the game, the parents of everybody on both teams got a call. "Would you please come down to the school library tomorrow evening at seven so we can resolve the issue? And bring your son."

Resolve the issue meant disqualify me so Springton would have a clear shot at the state championship.

Mom's eyes go glittery and that tight smile of hers froze her face and she said real sweet, "Oh yes, we'll be there. Thank you for calling." And I knew someone was in terminal trouble.

The Springton crowd hired a lawyer to do some research on the rules about where you had to live to play on a team, and they figured they'd just walk in there and this lawyer would read us the rules, and they'd smile and say, "Sorry," and I'd be ruled ineligible and they'd act real sad about the whole thing, and Springton would beat up on Mapleville the next day in the playoff, because I couldn't pitch.

Man, I mean, hiring a lawyer so you could stack the deck in favor of your home team? You'da thought we're talking major league world series!

What they didn't count on was my Mom.

When Mom finished the call that invited us to the war in the library, she banged the phone back on the receiver and stalked out of the house and was gone until the library closed, and she spent the next morning down there, too.

Seven oclock, everybody was seated in the library, and they were so polite it made you sick. Then about ten past seven Mr.

Patrick stands up and clears his throat, like it wasn't official unless he cleared his throat.

"I want to thank you all for coming. A little matter has come to the attention of the board of the little league about the rules of residence as they relate to what team a boy must play on."

What happens to guys when they get old? Why couldn't Patrick have just said, "Springton wants Joe knocked off the Mapleville team?"

Anyway, he turns to this lawyer with iron rimmed glasses and his hair parted dead center, and he says, "This is Mr. Peabody, an attorney we've hired to be certain of our ruling. Mr. Peabody is experienced in civic law and he will tell us about the rules."

Twenty minutes later Peabody concludes with, " . . and it appears to me that a player must live within the city limits of the team for which he intends to play. That being true, if Joseph Russell lives in the corporate limits of Springton, he can not play for Mapleville. I'm sorry." He shakes his head and smiles at me sadly and sits down.

Patrick stands up. "On the advice of the attorney, it appears Joe must play with Springton, or not at all."

Chairs scrape on the polished tile floor as eleven kids and twenty two parents from Mapleville stand up and for a minute I figure we're going to have a riot. EVERYBODY starts yelling at the same time and some parents are waving fists and pointing and threatening.

You know, let's just be real honest. Little league baseball isn't for the kids. It's for the parents so they can argue and hassle about everything and make perfect morons of themselves. If they'd have just asked the kids on both teams what's fair, they'd have all said, "Let Joe play with the team he started with," and that would have been fair, and the end of it, and forgotten. But no, the adults got to call a town meeting and hire a lawyer and get in everybody's face, and it's all going to be in the newspapers and talked about for years.

Well, anyway, Patrick finally thumps the table and tells everybody to take their seats and he says, "We have to abide by the rules."

Peabody nods yes, and looks at me with those sad eyes.

And then my Mom stands up and her eyes stop Patrick cold. She's smiling and she asks, "We have to abide the rules?"

Patrick knows Mom is about to kill him, but he doesn't know how.

"Why, yes. Of course."

Mom leans forward. "You do remember I called you two weeks ago about moving, and I asked you if it would be all right if Joe played for Mapleville after we moved. You do remember, don't you Mr. Patrick?"

His bald head goes red.

"Why, uh, umm, I remember a call."

"Now would you tell these people what you told me?"

"Well, uh, I don't exactly . . ."

"Mr. Patrick, Mapleville played the Panthers after that call. Do you remember?"

"Oh, yes, matter of fact they did, didn't they. Well, yes, I think I said it was okay for Joe to play for Mapleville, but you understand, I can't speak for the board."

"Oh?" Here comes that tight little smile. Mom opens a book.

"Matters concerning the rules will be ruled on by the board convened, except, the President of the league shall have power to make temporary rulings regarding residency and age of players which rulings shall be confirmed at the next convened board meeting and lacking such confirmation the ruling of the President shall become final."

She closes the book and I look at Patrick and he has just seen the Angel of Death.

"Mr. Patrick, the full board convened two days after I talked with you, and I have a copy of the minutes, and your temporary ruling was not on the agenda. Your ruling became final. You let Joe pitch against the Panthers and if you hadn't, the Panthers would have beaten Springton, and Mapleville would now be playing the Panthers, not Springton."

Man, that library was like a tomb.

Mom continues. "Since you didn't present your ruling to the full board at their next meeting convened, and you let him pitch against the Panthers, you can't stop him from pitching for Mapleville now."

Then, man oh man, she turns to Peabody and he's sitting there in a trance.

"Mr. Peabody, have you ever heard of "estoppel"? It's a legal term."

Peabody don't move a muscle.

I figure mom's talking Latin, about the plug you stick in the hole to keep water in a bathtub.

"I see you have," Mom says. "The league is estopped from making Joe change teams now."

The rest is history. I pitched and we beat Springton eight to two, and then we played a team from Bountiful, north of Salt Lake City and we beat them, and we took home the three foot trophy, and our coach had a smaller trophy made and gave it to Mom, and we went to Aurora and made it to the semifinals, but you know about that.

So here we are, the morning after the tryouts in our new town, and I hear Mom in the kitchen pushing all the Geezer's buttons.

"Ron, you can teach Joe how to bat. You know he's got a problem. It won't take much. Just a few minutes after work."

I mean, she said it like it would just take about twenty minutes after supper, and I'd know it all. Mom's like that. She can get anything done by pushing the right buttons on someone else, usually the Geezer.

"Yeah, okay," says the Geezer and he heads out the door to drive to work just as the phone rings.

Mom answers and she listens and nods. "Yes, he'll be there." She hangs up and turns to me.

"You're to be at the ball field at nine this morning so they can pick the teams."

This town takes Pony league baseball pretty serious, so they pick teams like a big league draft. The coaches show up and we stand around while they call out the names, and we negotiate and there's some trading until everyone says okay, and we got our teams.

Mom says she'll drive me but there's no way I'm going to let her be there, so I take my bicycle. I get there at nine o'clock and Shellins shows up five minutes later and everybody gathers by the backstop. The white shorts bunch are sort of together and they stand around looking like the other guys aren't there, and the other guys stand other places and try to look like they don't care that they aren't allowed to stand with the white short bunch.

I'm standing there alone in my blue full length Levi's and old beat up Nikes and an old short sleeved T-shirt, and I'm taking a blood oath with myself I'm never ever going to be caught dead in sissy white shorts, even if I have to leave home or join the Marines.

Shellins calls out, "Awright, all you guys get over there and wait, and all you coaches get over there and study these lists. We got seventy guys, just barely enough for seven teams and we only got one sub for each team."

We walk over by one dugout and Shellins and the other five coaches go to the other one and they huddle and start pointing and talking and I'm wondering, if we got enough for seven teams, why just six coaches.

"Awright," Shellins says, "coach with first pick, make your call."

This old guy with a pitted face and a mustache and a wad of tobacco in his jaw calls a name and a kid goes over and stands by him.

This goes on through five calls, and then Shellins makes his pick and then he coughs a little and he he says, "Since Coach Stern can't be here, he designated me to make his first pick, and I pick Mendoza."

I turn and whisper to the guy next to me, "What's that all about?"

"Coach Stern's in Japan on business. These guys are going to pick his team for him."

Yeah, right! And guess who they're going to pick.

Mendoza walks to where Shellins points, and he stands there alone and I look like I been hit in the head.

Mendoza's Hispanic and he stands about five foot four and he weighs 220 pounds if he weighs an ounce. His frame walks while everything else bounces. I mean, I figure that kid might be able to run the bases in about ten minutes if you let him stop at second base for a sandwich. There's one thing sure. Mendoza hasn't missed a meal since the day he was born. He's wearing bib overalls that are wore out at the knees and a button up shirt that has at least 3 buttons missing, and low cut old white sneakers he got from his grandpa. Mendoza just stares down at the ground while the snobby bunch gives him a look that says, disgusting.

I watch while the calls go on, and we come to the second call for Stern, and this time it's made by the coach with the mustache and tobacco.

"Chin."

A Chinese kid with a buzz haircut and $200 Reeboks turns to look when he hears his name and he's standing there with a blank face.

"Stand over there with Mendoza," Shellin says, but Chin don't move anything except his eyes, and they're everywhere.

Shellins frowns. "Stand over there," he says again, and he points.

The kid next to Chin whispers something to him and points, and Chin trots over and stands about ten feet from Mendoza. No closer.

I turn to the kid next to me and he whispers, "Chin don't talk English."

The call goes on and I don't recognize anyone except Leo Perry, a neat kid I met in church. I've talked baseball with him and he's good, and Leo got called out in the first round. I really hope I get on his team. Except for him, I don't know anything about anybody. I watch the teams start to take shape, and after about seven picks, I'm watching Stearn's team, and man, I'm feeling sorry for him. Two or three of the guys look like they might be fair, but the rest of them?

There's Mendoza, and Chin, and then there's this African American kid, about six foot three and so skinny he can't cast a shadow, and he's wearing white shorts and he's standing with Chin. From the look on his face I think think his IQ is about the same as his shoe size, which looks to be about fourteen. And there's this little kid about five feet, and with his mitt and cleats he might weigh eighty pounds, and he has quick moves, and he's standing near Mendoza. I figure if he puts a thirty two ounce Easton over his shoulder, he'll tip over backwards. Then there's one more kid that has all his baby fat and his cheeks are round and pink and his eyes squinty and I swear I smell talcum powder, and he's standing near the little quick kid.

The last round starts and the first six calls are made and I'm left standing there all alone and Shellins looks at me and then he goes over his list, and he says, "What was your name again?"

I shrug. "Joe Russell."

He looks at his list and he turns it over and looks and shakes his head. "You try out?"

"Yeah."

"We call you?"

"Yeah."

Shellins shrugs. "Okay. I'll have to check the tryout list. In the meantime you're on Stern's team."

I'm not on the list! I went through this stupid draft and I'm not on the list! While I wait, I take a look at Stern's team and it hits me! I got no choice! The only team without their tenth man is the one for coach Stern!

And I have never ever in my life seen, or heard of, or in my worst nightmare dreamed of, a bunch of misfit leftovers like these guys. I shake my head and walk over to Shellins, who's working with marked up rosters on a banged up old clip board.

I mumble, "I'm not on the list so just forget about it."

He shakes his head. "No, you're here on the tryout sheet. You were the last name and Irma just missed it when she typed. Teams got to have ten players to be legal and you're the tenth man so we got to have you."

And he lays it on me. "You're on Stern's team."

I look over at that gang and he reads my face, and he looks real irritated so I shrug and shuffle over to stand near Sterns collection of misfits.

Let me tell you, the words don't exist that will tell the rotten, horrible, sick, dead, please let me die feeling that I feel. I swallow and I look at the ground and I wish I was back home in Utah where nobody wore white shorts and nobody wound up on a baseball team that looked like this one.

Shellins comes back and bawls out, "Okay, listen up. You'll get a call later on telling you about practice times and game times, and where you play. Games start on time. You guys on Stern's team, he'll be back tonight and he wants you here tomorrow at five to get organized. That's it."

I grab my bike and I'm outta there, and I'm so shook every time I think of the Stern team that I nearly get myself killed in the traffic. I can't go home and tell Mom what happened. I just ride around for a long time and I don't even notice where I am. Finally I ride home and Mom's waiting.

"What's wrong?" Moms can tell when something's wrong while you're still a mile away.

"Nothin'."

"Tell me what's wrong."

I shrug. "Nothin'."

"You didn't get on Leo's team?"

I shake my head.

"What team are you on?"

"Stern's."

"Oh. He's the one that's gone?"

"Yeah." How did she know that? Easy. Moms know everything. Voices tell them while they sleep at night.

"How did the team look?"

"Disaster."

She puckers her face. "Can't be that bad. Lunch is on the table."

How can she do that? I mean, my life has just been ruined and she's talking about tuna fish sandwiches and soup.

After lunch she makes me do some yard work and then I have some free time and I lock myself in my room and my mind quits working every time I think about the Geezer coming home, and I start thinking of where I'll go when I run away from home.

The Geezer comes home and Mom's busy fixing supper, and the Geezer disappears into the garage with a box he brought home and after a few minutes comes out and sticks his head in the front door and calls me. I walk into the front yard and he's standing beside a batting tee. A baseball on a long elastic cord is anchored to it and the Geezer has a new Louisville thirty ounce bat.

I close my eyes and roll my head. Not again.

See, the Geezer was my team coach three years ago and he just kept drilling us kids on what he called the fundamentals.

"When you throw, throw at the man's numbers. When you field a ball, drop to one knee. When you bat, keep your head down and watch the ball until you make contact. Don't try to kill it. Just meet it. Hit singles. You win ball games with singles. Play a mental game."

Then he'd run us through skull drills. That's where he would give you a set up, like, "a man is on third and there's one out and the batter hits a grounder to the second baseman. What's the play?" And he'd jab a finger at one of us and we had to have the answer.

I played tee ball when I was five and I've used a batting tee for the past six years, and he made all of us on the team use it three years ago when he coached, and now he thinks he's going to show me how it works? World class boredom! I heave a sigh and start for the door.

He stops me. "Okay, Joe," he says, "What was your batting average last year?"

"I don't remember."

".268. I'll make you a deal."

"Yeah?"

"Do what I tell you and I guarantee you a .350 or better batting average."

I mean, I've heard dumb and I've heard stupid but that's high grade insanity.

"Yeah. Right," I say. "You showed me before."

He looks a little sad and says, "Yeah, but you're older. Better coordinated. Okay. Head down. Watch the ball until you make contact. Swing level. That's to start with. When you can hit the ball ten times in a row without hitting the tee, call me."

He swings one slow to show me, and then he takes a regular swing, and I got to admit, for a Geezer fifty six years old and six foot four and two hundred forty pounds, you can tell he's done it before, probably when he was a kid just after the Mayflower landed at Plymouth Rock. Half an hour later I walk into the house, sweating. "I done it."

He walks back out with me and stands by the tee and says, "Fine. Now take ten swings and I count the times you hit rubber."

I hit the ball cleanly eight out of ten.

He takes the bat and hits it cleanly eight out of ten.

"Tie," he said. "We go again."

We go through that four times in a row, him hitting as many as I did.

"Okay. Now we move on. You watch my arms."

He goes real slow. "Okay, right here, when you make contact with the ball, your right arm's stiff and pushing and your left one's pulling, just before you roll your wrists to complete the swing. The power is in that snap, right there, just before you roll your wrists. Hitting isn't all muscle. Little guys can hit just as hard as big ones if they learn to make make that snap just before they roll their wrists, and when you do it right you'll feel it clear down through your hips. Real power is technique, not muscle. Okay, you do it."

"Yeah, yeah."

I step up and swing.

"No, Joe, go slow. Do it slow twenty times. Just like I showed you. Head down. Eyes on the ball. Swing slow. Learn to roll your wrists on the follow through. Go again."

He watches for a few minutes. "Okay, its coming. Stay with it." He walks back into the house.

Sure sure. When he disappears I haul back and rip away and nearly knock the batting tee over.

Then I settle down. I mean, if I do everything he tells me and it still turns out wrong, then he's the one who blew it. Right? I mark it in my head. When I'm batting .150 this summer, he's going to hear about it.

Half an hour later they call me for supper.

I bolt the food down and excuse myself and trot back out.

They call me for bed later on when it gets dark. My shirt is soaked through with sweat and my arms and wrists ache. We just get through with family prayer when the phone rings and it's Shellins.

"Your team is called the Reds. First practice is tomorrow at five and Coach Stearn will be there, and the first game is next day at Griffith field."

First practice tomorrow and a game the next day?

These guys are crazy!

THE FIRST PRACTICE - DISASTER!

I BICYCLE TO GRIFFITH A
little early and I'm standing off away from the backstop when
this silver Mercedes Benz stops and the tall skinny African
American kid gets out of the back seat and he's still wearing
those dumb white shorts. I'm still wearing my Sears winter
special sale Levi's.

Then a new red Chrysler pulls in and that little kid with the
quick moves climbs out.

A black Lincoln limo half a block long stops and the Chinese
kid with the buzz gets out, and from the size of that limo I figure he's already been practicing baseball inside.

Then Mendoza peddles up on a beat up old bicycle with one
fender, and a seat from a kids tricycle.

Two guys get out of a Suburban and walk on over, and another kid rides up on his bicycle.

Pretty soon eight of us are there, and I stand off to one side
working on the pocket in my mitt, and the guys that arrived in
Limo's and Cadillacs and white shorts are standing together,
and the guys that got here on bicycles and in Suburbans are off
to one side, and Mendoza's standing alone.

Then this blue Toyota pickup drives up and a guy gets out
and he's about average size, and has a nose that resembles a par-

rot's beak and makes his face look sort of sharp and pointy. I mean, he isn't bad looking, it just looks like everything else is there to support his nose. One of the kids I don't know gets out the other side and walks around and they grab a big bag of equipment from the back of the truck and walk over to the dugout.

Another guy drives up and gets out and the kid with the fat pink cheeks gets out with him, and they walk over to the dugout and the first guy and the second guy start talking and pulling bats and catcher's protective stuff out of the bag.

We're all there, and I know, I absolutely know, that there's no chance this bunch of mismatch-misfits is going to make a ball team. I mean, we're already divided into bunches, rich kids and not rich kids. This gang is nowhere.

We don't have real dugouts. They're just benches behind chain link fences that run halfway down the first and third base lines, and they connect up with the backstop. Anyway, the nose guy signals us and we all sit down on a bench.

"I'm Jesse Stern," he says. "I'm your coach. We're the Reds, and we're going to have a great season."

He's crazy! He looks normal but he's crazy!

"This is my assistant coach, Milt Briggs."

The second guy stands up and gives us a once over. He's pretty good size and a nice looking guy with sandy hair.

Briggs sits down and coach goes on. "I'm sorry I missed the draft yesterday but I had to be in Japan for the international convention of psychologists."

This guy's a psychologist! I quietly close my eyes and pray for a monster earthquake. We got a bunch of rejects for players, and a psychologist for a coach. I mean, a truck driver or a hobo or a steel worker or a bum or anything but a psychologist. I seen these guys on tv and they're all nuts. This has got to be the all time worst nightmare ever inflicted on the sport of baseball. THE All Time.

"Okay, here's my rules. We play hard. We play together. We don't complain. We do our best. If we do our best we win, no matter what the score is. We compliment the other team. We don't contest umpire decisions. We don't use bad language. We are gentlemen."

My mouth drops open. He found these rules on some other planet. I mean, you got to have some things or baseball isn't baseball. Like hassling the other team. There are two languages. English and Baseball. Coaches and players stand in front of a mirror at home at night and practice mean expressions, and how to grind insults through clenched teeth. You haven't played the game right if you don't give the other team fits.

Who's worried about winning a game? We know we're going to lose every one, and all that leaves us is doing our job of name calling and being mean, and now this jerk's taking that away.

"Okay, we got seven teams, the A's, Angels, Orioles, Cubs, Cardinals, Blue Jays, and us, the Reds. Here's the schedule. We play the season in two halves, six games to the half. The team with most wins after six games wins that half, and the same for the second half. If the same team wins both halves, they're the champs. If not, the two winners play it off for league championship. Okay. Everybody stand up and say your name."

The African American kid is Bernie Billman. Then Mendoza and Chin. The pink cheeked kid is Ned Briggs, the assistant coach's kid, and he catches. The kid that arrived with the coach is Jackie Stern, the coach's kid, and he pitches. There's two brothers, one shy, the other not, and their names are Randy and Denny Stott. The little guy that moves quick is Rockland and they call him Stone, and the last one is Scott Webb.

I'm last and I stand and mumble, "Joe Russell."

Coach looks at me. "What position?"

"Pitch. And field."

"Which one most?"

"Pitch."

"All right. Let's get started. Infielders scatter out on the base paths and outfielders go with Briggs out to catch some flies. Joe, you go with the outfield."

I pick my mitt from between my feet and trot out to center field with some others, and Briggs picks up a bat and we start taking turns at catching flies. Bernie lines up on one side of me, Mendoza on the other, and I'm surprised when I look at

23

Bernie close up. I'm just under six feet tall, and he's about six three, but it seems like he's a lot taller than that. I think it's because he's so skinny. He looks like a bunch of tinker toys, with sticks for arms and legs, and knobs for knees and elbows. He looks at me suspicious and don't say anything.

Briggs calls my name and smacks one and I mosey over and take it and throw. He calls Bernie and hits, and Bernie gets all those tinker toys moving the same direction, and he makes the catch and he throws back, pretty strong, and I raise an eyebrow in surprise, and he looks at me like he's a real cool dude. Briggs calls Mendoza and hits it right to him and Mendoza has this ratty old mitt and he takes dead aim and waits with his mouth open while the ball arches down. He misses it and it hits him right in the forehead. He smiles like it's okay, and tries to pick it up, and he boots it and finally surrounds it, and he underhands it and it goes nowhere and I pick it up and relay it on in.

Between my turns catching flies, I keep an eye on the infield and the guys warming up to pitch, and there is absolutely nothing there. In a while coach calls us all together and tells us its time for a few fungoes to the infield, and we'll rotate at bat.

He says, "Jackie on the mound, and Ned behind the plate," and I wonder why I'm not surprised. The rest of us fan out in the infield. Chin takes first, Stone takes third, and the shy Stott brother takes short stop, and the rest of us fill in the holes.

Jackie throws easy and coach hits grounders, and we go around once, and then Chin takes the bat and we all rotate one position towards first, except Jackie and Ned stay on the mound and behind the plate.

Anyway, it goes on, and then coach calls, "Okay, you guys take full positions. Jackie, bear down and Milt's going to hit away."

The guys spread, some in the outfield, four in the infield. Jackie nods and starts giving us the best stuff he's got. It's, you know, okay, but it hasn't got that 'pop.' Briggs raps out some hot grounders and some to us in the outfield. We go on for about fifteen minutes and coach calls, "Joe, warm up with Chin. You're next on the mound."

I stop dead for a minute and then I walk over into the shade of some trees back of the third base line and Chin comes over and drops into the catcher's crouch, and I start throwing easy. He's catching and tossing back pretty good, but this guy's a little scary. From the time he got out of that aircraft carrier limo, I haven't seen him change expression or say a word other than his name once, and there's a sort of a hint of smile and the black eyes behind those half closed eyelids are always shifting from one thing to another, like Chin knows something bad and he's not telling.

"Okay, Joe," coach says, "take the mound."

I walk out there onto the top of the mound and I toe the rubber, and man, that special feeling comes right on up from my shoes to my hat, and I know - that's the center of the universe. I turn to face the batter and it's the Stott brother who's not shy. He's built good and he takes his stance and waits.

I look at Ned back there with the chest protector and the mask and I wait for a sign but he doesn't give me one, so I let go a fastball. The Stott kid doesn't move and it smacks into Ned's glove for a strike and Ned drops it because he can't handle it.

He picks it out of the dirt and throws it back and I wait for the signal again and Ned don't move so I rear back and deliver another fast ball. It whacks into Ned's glove and Stott swings, way too late. Ned's mouth forms a little "oooooo" and he slips his hand out of his mitt and shakes it a time or two before he puts the mitt back on.

Ned still doesn't give me a sign so I chuck another fast ball and Stott swings too late again, and when the ball smacks into Ned's glove you can hear it clear out to the rest rooms, two hundred yards away. Things go kind of quiet and no one moves.

Coach takes his hands out of his pockets and looks, and says, "Throw one more," sort of easy and breezy.

I deliver and Stott watches it go past and it smacks, and Ned grits his teeth and slips his hand out of the mitt and shakes it a little.

"Nice, Joe, nice," coach says, "got a curve?"

World's all time dumb question. Have I got a curve?

I crank up and deliver and the ball comes in head high before it starts off to the left, and dropping. Stott swings, and he misses about eighteen inches, and Ned's glove touches the dirt on the outside of the plate when he catches it. The infield is standing with their hands at their sides, not moving, and coach Briggs' head is hanging forward while his eyes pop.

Coach turns. "Ned, take the mound, Bernie, you come catch. That's all for now, Joe."

I walk back to the bench.

"You played center field?", Stern asks.

He sends me out to replace Bernie.

Pretty soon a station wagon pulls into the asphalt parking lot east of the field and a woman with a bandana holding back her hair gets out and coach yells, "Uniforms are in," and we all go to the station wagon. We get white pants just like all the other teams, but each team gets a different colored shirt. Ours are red.

"Everybody got one that fits?," coach asks, and we all mumble yeah.

"Have your mom wash it for the game tomorrow. Be here at four-thirty for warmup. Game starts at five. You're late without a good excuse, you can't play. I'll have the starting lineup posted."

Yeah, right. With one coach's kid a pitcher and the other a catcher, guess who pitches and catches. Jackie threw about forty today. I threw five.

Politics.

I roll up the uniform and slip the strap on my mitt over the bicycle handlebar and tuck the roll under my arm, and I peddle on home. Mom's in the kitchen humming and finishing supper and the car's there so the Geezer's home somewhere, but I go straight to my room. Pretty soon Mom calls for supper and I go wash and walk on out to the table.

She's made meatloaf, and I mean she's the undisputed world champ meatloafer - and tapioca pudding with chocolate syrup - my favorite dessert. I have trouble with tapioca pudding after the sixth bowl, but the first six bowls are pure heaven.

I sit down and she doesn't really look at me, but she knows.

"Bad practice?," she asks.

"What practice?"

She stops. "That bad?"

I shake my head. "Don't ask."

She walks back to the kitchen for the plate of baked potatoes, and the Geezer gives me a look, and I know what's going to happen before I get to bed. Sooner or later.

Supper's a study in Mom acting cheerful and me sitting under a cloud of gloom, and I can't get past the third bowl of tapioca pudding, and I mumble an excuse and go to my room. I'm sitting there on my bed, slumped against the wall, when this rap comes.

I know who it is. "Yeah."

The Geezer walks in.

I don't move.

He sits down on my study chair, in front of my desk. "Not so good, huh?"

"Terminal."

"What happened?"

"The coach is a psychologist." That ought to explain the whole thing.

"What about the team?"

"Zeroes."

"You get to throw any?"

"Five."

"How'd it go?"

I shrug. "Okay. Won't do no good."

"Why."

"The coach's kid pitches and the assistant's kid catches."

The Geezer drops his eyes and studies his knuckles for a while. "You getting home towned?"

"Royal."

He shakes his head and I can see pain in his eyes. "Well, that's the way it goes. Life's full of it. What you going to do about it?"

"Nothing."

"Then that's how your season's going to go. Nothing."

Why doesn't he understand? Always, always, a lecture. I look at him kind of smarty and I say, "Okay, you tell me what to do."

"Figure out where you can win."

"I did. There's no place I can win"

"Yeah, there is. You can't pick your team mates, and you can't decide who pitches, so you can't win there. But you can decide to give it all you got wherever you are. You can decide you're going to improve your batting. You can decide to give those other guys all your support. Figure out what part of it you can control, and give it everything. That can be your win."

I'm so tired of him and his crappy philosophy stuff that don't have nothing to do with the problem. I shake my head and I can feel my temper.

"Yeah, right, big deal. A neat fielder who yells great things to the worst team in town. I'll look like a dork out there."

The Geezer sighs. "No you won't. It sounds like the team needs a leader. That could be you."

"LEADER! I'd rather have cancer. You couldn't pay me to be their leader."

The Geezer slowly stands. "You better make up your mind pretty soon, or this is going to be a long summer." He stands there a minute like he wants to say more but he doesn't, and he looks a little sad when he walks out.

The sick stomach feeling rises inside, and I'm glad he's gone, and I hate that feeling. He thinks he has all the answers to everything, but he's forgotten the pain of the turmoil that tears at your insides and the feeling of being lost in an ocean of mixed up feelings that you don't understand, and you don't know which way to go.

Our team is going to be used for target practice by all the other teams. I'm going to be the kid that got to pitch after the coach's kid got through, and our team will be famous for turning in a perfect season. Lost every game.

So the Geezer walks out of my bedroom and I settle on my bed with my back against the wall and my sick stomach comes back, like always, and I sit there and I say nothing because there's no way it's ever going to be different.

And at that moment I hate baseball, and the Geezer, and this town.

FIRST GAME - FREAKY WIN

I LAY IN BED UNTIL AFTER nine o'clock and wait for Mom because I know she'll come, and when she walks in I don't move. She puts her hand on my forehead and says, "You feeling well?"

I make my voice croaky and I stare at the ceiling and I say, "I'll be okay."

"Sounds like you've caught cold."

I talk croaky some more and say, "No, I'll be okay."

"Say aahhhhh."

I open and say aahhhhh.

"Throat's not red," she says. She puts her hands on her hips and her face puckers and she says, "Well, you stay in bed. If you're not better by this afternoon I'll call your coach."

She walks out and I breathe easier. She bought it. Mom comes back in ten minutes with a glass of steaming lemonade with a lot of sugar and I take my time and drink it slow. When she comes back for the glass I lay here with my back to the door and look like I'm asleep and she takes the glass and sneaks out so she won't wake me.

At one o'clock she brings in toast and cottage cheese and the rest of the tapioca pudding from last night, and milk. At four o'clock the Geezer comes home early for the game, and I hear him walk in the door just as the phone rings, and he takes it. He listens for a minute and says he'll call back and he asks Mom, "Where's Joe?"

She tells him and he walks into my room and I look at him and I can tell he's got all his radar up, and I get this sick stomach again.

"You sick?"

I try to talk croaky like before but this time it doesn't sound right. "No, I'm okay."

"Mother says you've been sick. Caught cold?"

"I don't think so."

He walks over and clamps that paw of his on my forehead, closes his eyes to concentrate, and moves it down to my cheek for a few seconds. "Open your mouth."

He stares into my throat. "No temperature, no red. What's wrong?"

"I told Mom, nothing."

"You throw up today?"

"No."

"That was your coach on the phone. The two Stott brothers are down in Chino with their dad and he's had a fender bender car wreck and they can't be back until about five thirty. The team can start with eight players, but if you're not there, that leaves seven, and the team has to forfeit."

I feel the grab in the pit of my stomach.

"Get dressed. We'll go to the hospital emergency room."

He starts for the door and I sit up and say, "No, I'll go. If I get worse I'll come home after the Stott kids get there."

I get dressed and we drive to Griffith in the family's old Chevy and I slump down because the Geezer parks between a Mercedes and a Cadillac. I wait until I'm sure nobody's looking and I get out and walk fast to the bench. Coach comes and we all sit down.

"I know we haven't had time to practice much, but neither have they. Just remember my rules. We get the field first. Go warm up."

We trot out and I go to the outfield with Bernie and Mendoza because I figure I'll be in the outfield. Briggs knocks us flies for ten minutes, and coach calls us back, and the other team takes the field for their ten minute warmup, and I lean against the chainlink and watch.

"Joe." I turn and it's coach calling.

"Go throw to Ned. You're starting on the mound."

I stand there forever with my mouth open before I can believe it. I look at him like he's made a mistake and he gives me a hand signal to get moving. I go out in the shade behind third base and Ned grins and shows me a thick leather shoe half sole he stuck in his mitt since yesterday. I start to throw to him, soft and easy.

The Geezer has lectured me about my arm until I can't stand it. "You feel a pain, a twinge, a pull, - anything - you tell the coach and you're out of there." He says too many pitchers are finished before they start because they don't respect their arm. Even if you warm up good, your arm gets sore, and I've felt the pain and ache plenty of times, so I throw easy until its all loose and warm.

I glance at the bleachers and the Geezer's there, watching the team, turning to glance at me once in a while. I silently pray that he doesn't cut loose with his rebel yell today. You can hear it all over the field, and everybody stops to see who did it. I look at him like, who's that nutty old guy, but everybody knows it's the Geezer, and he's my Dad, and I have to live with it.

We play the A's today, and they finish their warmup and trot over to their bench, and turn to look at what I've got. I'm throwing light so they won't know.

If you know baseball, you know a lot of people don't have a clue. It isn't one guy throwing a ball as hard as he can while the other guy with the bat tries to knock the cover off of it. You got to keep track of a hundred things about the batters, and the park, and even where the sun is. Major leaguers keep books on guys, and pitchers and catchers memorize them so you know what kind of pitch each guy likes and doesn't like.

You don't try to strike everybody out. You got to pitch smart, and learn to set guys up. Like, a fastball inside to move a batter back, then a big looping curve on the outside edge and he has to reach to get it and he taps a dribbler to the shortstop and gets thrown out at first. People think, that's a lousy pitcher because the shortstop had to save him. Fact is, that's exactly how the pitcher figured it, and those who understand know he's really good.

Or, you got a heavy duty slugger looking at you, and you throw him a changeup on the outside edge of the plate, and he lunges and hits it a little low and it pops real high to the outfield and is caught. People think, man, that pitcher isn't very good - that guy nearly hit a home run. Fact is, that's just how the pitcher figured it.

You got to learn to get ahead of the batter, which means of the first three pitches, two got to be strikes. That way, the batter don't dare let a close one go by, and they swing at almost anything within reach of the plate.

There's a scary side, too. You pitch long enough, you're going to have some days when it all goes wrong, and on those days it don't matter who you are, there isn't a thing you can do about it. You just have a crappy, crummy day and you go home and grump and storm around the house.

So, I'm looking over at the A's, and I haven't got a clue about who can hit and what pitches they like. I don't even know what finger signals Ned uses.

I walk over to Ned. "You know these guys?"

"A little." His face is white.

"Okay. Let's keep it simple. One finger, fast ball. Two fingers, a curve. Three fingers, a sinker. We'll start with just those. Okay?"

"Got it."

The umpire - we call them the "blues" because they wear blue shirts - brushes off home plate with his pocket whisk broom, and turns to face both benches.

"Reds are home team and they field first. Take your positions."

Umpires look like Sumo wrestlers because they wear padding underneath their shirts, and then they have the big padded chest protector outside. We all know about the padding, but it still cuts down on arguments, because they look like a Tiger Tank standing there.

I toss a couple of easy ones to Ned and when I get the ball back I start to rub it while I take a walk around the mound and look at our players. We only got two outfielders because the

Stott brothers haven't come yet. Bernie's out there, and Mendoza. Then we got Stone on third, Jackie at short, Webb on second, Chin at first, and me and Ned. I notice Chin's got a big handbook that bulges his hip pocket.

I quit rubbing the ball and step onto the mound and I take my standard eight throws for real. The arm's okay. Not great, but okay.

"Batter up," shouts the blue and puts his mask on and crouches over behind Ned.

Coaches usually put three good hitters up first, then a long ball clean-up hitter to get them home if any of them get on base. So this first guy is supposed to be one of their good hitters.

I stand there and wait and finally Ned tucks his hand down there between his legs and gives me the signal. One finger.

I crank up and I deliver a belt high fast ball right down the center of the plate and the batter don't move. He just stands there until it smacks into Ned's glove and Ned winces a little.

The blue turns and pumps his right arm and hollers "Steerike."

Their coach comes off their bench and shoves his face against the chain link to get a better look.

I wait for Ned and he signs one finger again.

This one comes in three inches higher than the last one but still in the strike zone, right where I intended and this kid at bat don't move until it smacks into Ned's mitt, and then he licks his lips and he looks at the bat, sort of lost, like he can't figure out how he got to the ballfield. Or maybe he can't figure out *why* he got to the ballfield.

I wait and Ned signs two fingers and I crank up this curve, and this kid's waiting for another fastball and the curve starts to break and he swings and it breaks more and he tries to correct his swing, and he goes down too far and the end of his bat digs dirt and it knocks it out of his hands and it skitters off towards first base.

Ned cracks a little smile and those slitty little eyes of his go nearly shut as the blue gives another right jab and hollers, "Steerrike" and the kid starts for the bench and then remembers the bat and he trots over and gets it and walks to the bench. Their next two batters come up, and I throw six more pitches, and the top of the first is history - three strikeouts.

The guys on their bench are like statues and their coach is standing with his face against the chain link, his nose stuck through one of the holes.

We hear someone yell from the parking lot and look over there and the Stott brothers are running towards us. Coach walks out to me.

"You still sick? Want to go home?"

I shake my head. "Nope. I'm better." I don't dare look at the Geezer or mom.

Coach puts Randy and Denny Stott on the line-up and shows the blue and gives a copy to the other coach. Mendoza goes to the bench, Denny Stott goes to the outfield, Jackie goes to the outfield, and Randy Stott - the sad eyed one - goes to short stop. I notice Chin sitting at the end of the bench with his nose buried in that book from his rear pocket, and I casually walk past and look, and it's a translation book! Chinese to English and back to Chinese. I mean, we got a guy that has to look up words to know what's going on! I shake my head, but there's no time to think about it.

Our lead off man is Ned.

I watch while he steps up to the plate and settles his feet into the dirt.

Third pitch, he connects and drops a nice little pop over the second baseman's head that drops into center field for a single.

Second batter is Randy. Second pitch, he connects, right down the third base line into left field. Ned scampers around to third, Randy stops on first.

Third batter is Chin. Pops out.

Fourth batter is Bernie. Clean up batter. I figure the coach has lost his mind. Bernie a hitter? All those tinker toys?

Second pitch, he smacks one out between center and left field and both Ned and Randy score and Bernie holds up on second. The whole team looks at him from the dugout and he's standing there all smug and snobby, like, well, what else did you expect, and I yell "Way to go" but nobody else on the team yells anything and I look around and shut up. This bunch doesn't doesn't have a clue about the meaning of the word "team."

Our next batter is thrown out at first and the one after him strikes out. Bottom of the first is history, but we got two runs.
I trot back to the mound to warm up again and I stop to rub the ball and I look at our infield, and they all look sort of puzzled, surprised.

Ned starts his signs, and nine pitches later the top of the second is history, three more strike outs. The last two batters went down swinging but I don't think either one of them knew what they swung at. I think their coach just told them don't worry about whether it's a curve or fastball, just swing. Do that enough and sooner or later someone is going to connect.

Bottom of the second, we go down one, two, three. I'm number two. I strike out and the Geezer sees how it gets to me. I look away from him because I don't want one of his silent lectures.

I go back to the mound and Ned signs curve and ten pitches later the top of the third is over. Two strike outs, and one thrown out at first. The guy who hit it had both eyes closed when he swung and he hit a dribbler to Randy.

Bottom of the third, we go down leaving two on base.

Top of the fourth, we're still ahead, two to zero. I rub the ball and take another look at our infield and they still look like they don't know what's going on.

I strike out the first batter and the second and third batters hit dribbly balls, one to second base and one to Stone at third and they throw out the batters at first base.

So far, we've put down their batters one, two, three, every inning. I really haven't got all my stuff together in top form, but it's good enough. I feel good. Ned's starting to act like he has a little more confidence.

We take our turn at bat and I'm the second batter again. This time when I pick up the bat the Geezer stands up in the bleachers for just a moment and it catches my eye. All he does is tip his head forward and look down and he's giving me one of his famous silent lectures - keep your head down and watch the ball until you make contact. I just purely hate those silent lectures.

35

I keep my head down and watch the ball and it happens just like I know it will. A called strike.

Second pitch, I swing and hit a blooper over the first baseman and it drops for a single. Pure accident. The next two batters go down and leave me stranded.

Two innings later I get up again and I keep my head down and I crack a hard liner over the second baseman and it drops for a single. Again I get stranded, but I got my second hit. Freak accident.

We move to the top of the seventh and I rub up the ball while I circle the mound, and I take a second to size things up. The score's still two to zip. If we can hold on for just three more outs, this bunch of nobody misfits has won the first game. Not only that, but we will have a no hitter! I look at the guys and they still got that far away look in their eyes.

First batter comes up, Ned signs, and three pitches later the kid's dragging his bat back to the bench.

Second batter comes up and Ned signs for an inside fastball and I deliver and it moves the batter back a few inches, and next pitch is on the outside edge and he lunges and pops a slow bouncer out to Randy at short stop and I watch it and it's a lazy, Sunday afternoon bouncer that you can handle with your eyes closed.

Randy fields it with no sweat, and he transfers the ball smooth from his mitt to his throwing hand, and he cocks and throws and I see it's too high and I stand there helpless while it sails clear over Chin's head, out by a big cottonwood behind first base. Chin sprints but he barely gets there before the kid pulls up on second, safe.

And right there, I can smell it coming. This bunch is going to blow it. The tieing run is coming up, and I can see it in the faces of our guys. They somehow knew they were going to mess up this game.

Their next batter comes up and I can see this kid's in trouble. I think his coach has told him to hit anything. Just get a hit. Score that guy from second.

So I fire a fast ball strike past him and then a ball and then another fast ball strike and he hears the blue yell "Steerike", and I'm way ahead of him and he knows it, and he looks at his coach and his coach's face is a screwed up snarl, and this kid looks back at me with pure panic.

I come out of my windup and my arm comes over and I see this kid with his eyes clamped shut and he's got every muscle in his body swinging the bat, blind. It seems to me like we're in slow motion while I watch the ball make a line towards the center of the plate, and the bat coming around, and I can tell they're going to collide and then the bat hits the ball dead center.

With these aluminum bats, you can tell how hard a ball is hit by the sound. A nice, average hit is a "tink." A heavy duty hit is a "tank." And a granddaddy hit is a "tunk."

This guy gets a strong "tank" and I watch the ball leave the bat and it's a screamer, headed towards third, to Stone's left. I just see a streak as the ball comes past me and I think, dive for a hole, Stone, you're too light for that one.

I can't believe my eyes. This teeny tiny little guy makes a lunge and a stab and spears the ball, and the runner from second stops and he can't believe it and for just a minute he stands there and then makes a dive back for the base to tag up.

Now this is where things get crazy. When the ball smacks into Stone's glove it whips him into a complete three hundred sixty degree turn that's so fast all we can see is his mitt sticking out of this blur. He does a second three sixty and this time we see his other hand suddenly flick out and the ball snaps over to second base like a bullet. The runner from second hits the ground and his hand slaps the bag just a microsecond before the ball whacks into Webb's glove. The guy's safe, but I can't believe that great play by Stone.

Stone? After the third three sixty he slows down and starts to stagger around dizzy for a minute and then he starts to hop up and down on one foot and then the other with his mitt between his legs like he's trying to pull it off and can't. The only sound we hear is sort of a prolonged whine while he's hopping and jerking his hand.

I call time and trot over. "You okay?"

He slows down his hopping and jerking and looks at me in surprise like he doesn't know where he is.

"Sure."

"You spin like that all the time?"

"No, only once in a while."

"Why do you do that?"

"Leverage to throw."

"Let me see your hand." I figure it must be broken. I see the coach trotting out to us.

"Can't."

"Why?"

"Can't get the mitt off."

That doesn't surprise me. I figure the ball fused the mitt to his hand. I see him trying to eat supper that night with his mitt on his hand and at the hospital next morning where a team of surgeons removes the mitt.

The coach breaks through the ring. "Stone," he says, "you all right?"

"Me? Oh yeah, coach. I'm great." I know he can't feel a thing below his elbow on his left arm.

"Shall we get Mendoza in here for the rest of the game?"

"Naw. I'm fine. Let's play ball." He smacks his right hand into the mitt like usual and acts like he's getting set to play again. The coach nods and we all trot back to our positions.

On the mound I stop again to rub the ball and turn around and look at the guys. I look at Stone and something inside me turns over and I think to myself, crazy, but gutsy, real gutsy. I look at the other guys and they still got that weird look in their eyes like something's wrong and nobody's yelling anything to Stone.

Stone got us the second out and we got one more to go. I look at the batter coming up and I shake off Ned's sign for a curve and I take a fastball sign, and I crank up a fastball that hits Ned's mitt with a smack that you can hear clear out in the parking lot.

I shake off another curve sign and deliver another fastball, and this guy takes strike two, called.

He looks at me and he's saying, one more. Just give me one more.

So I do.

He swings after it hits Ned's mitt and it's over and we won it, two zip, and it's a no hitter shutout.

People in the bleachers are yelling, and the other team's standing around sort of dazed, and this nutty thing is happening with my guys. I expect them to come charging in, yelling their heads off "WE WON WE WON" but they don't. They come in sort of trotting and walking and they're making a little noise but not much, and they're looking at each other and then at their parents in the bleachers, and like they don't quite know what to do.

I look at them and I say to Randy, "What's the deal? We won."

Randy shrugs and then I figure it out.

They don't know how to act! I knew the rich kids and the other kids were divided, and that's part of it, but it about knocks me cold when I realize these guys came expecting to lose, and we won, and now they got two problems. How do you mix rich guys with not rich guys, and then how do they act when they knew they were going to lose, but they won?

They can't figure that all out, and they're standing around kind of like they're lost, or dazed.

Someone finally yells and then they all yell a little, but you know, it isn't that wild sort of loud yell that says we're a team and we can lick any team in town. I slap Stone on the back for his helicopter routine, and I jerk his mitt off and his hand is still white like the blood is scared to come back, but it isn't broke.

Randy says, "Nice game, Joe", but that's all I get for throwing a shut out, but that doesn't bother me because I figure Stone is the one who deserves it. I mean, this little runty guy had no business grabbing that bullet.

We go back onto the infield and walk through the usual line with the other team, giving them the high five as they pass. They don't say a word, because they can't believe they got beat by this mis-matched bunch of nobodies.

I know the rest of the season isn't going to be this easy, because most of the coaches for the other teams were in the bleachers scouting us and the word is going to get out. I figure this is going to be the only game we'll win.

But at least we won the first one. Eleven losses and one win on the season is better than twelve straight losses, which is what we figured when we started.

"Good game, fellows," says Stern. "Stone, that was a good play in the seventh."

Stone grins and nods.

"Practice tomorrow at six p.m.," Coach says. "Everybody be here. Here's the schedule for the rest of the season," and he hands out schedules.

We all start to gather our stuff. Coach walks over to me and holds the big green sack while I drop the batting helmets in.

"Good game, Joe. Thank you."

I just keep tossing helmets into the green bag.

On the drive home the Geezer starts his humming and I think I'm in for the unbounded pain of another poem. But he just says, "Two for four. That's .500."

I think, if he starts a lecture about how I got my two hits by keeping my head down and looking, the way he said I should, I'm going to get out and walk.

"Pure accident. Dumb luck," I say.

He just hums some more and I slump down in the seat of our four year old Chevy as the black aircraft carrier Lincoln limo passes us.

THE COACHS' BIG SURPRISE

"JOE, THE YARD AND SHRUBS."
I look up from my breakfast pancakes and nod as the Geezer leaves for work. I spend the morning and early afternoon pushing the lawnmower and running the trimmer, and about three forty five I head on down to Griffith. Our next game's against the Blue Jays, and the schedule said they practice at four today, just ahead of us, and I want to see what they got.

You got to plan each game like a general, and you got to consider everything. Griffith Park is beautiful, I mean, flowers and trees and stuff, and natural grass like a carpet, but that means a ball rolls slower than on artificial turf.

There's two fields, north and south, and we play mostly on the north field, and it faces a little south and east. That means in late afternoon the team in the field is looking west and they got sun in their eyes. There's no fences, and that means you can't knock a ball over a fence and call it a home run. You got to hit it so far the fielders can't get there and throw it back into play. And you got to know which guys on the other team hits long and short, so you'll know when to play deep or shallow, and whether they hit left or right, so you can sag your players that direction. The Geezer says it's like life. It's a crazy game. You do everything right and you lose, you do everything wrong and you win. Next time you do it right and win, do it wrong and you lose. You love it and you hate it and you can never be sure of it and you can never quit.

So I'm way out there in some trees by the parking lot, watching, and it doesn't take long to get the message.

These guys are scary. I mean, their coach calls them all together and gives them a two minute wake up call, and this bunch moves out fast. They field, and they steal and slide, and hit and run, and then he calls them in for batting practice, and he spends half an hour on bunting.

I think about that for a minute. He's scouted our game last night and he knows his guys aren't going to get many good hits off me, so he's going to have them bunt.

He spends a few minutes on hitting away, and he's out there telling them, head down, eye on the ball, watch until it makes contact, don't swing for the fence, just meet it, and this guy knows baseball, and these guys are soaking it up like sponges.

They take full field positions for the last while, and call out a pitcher named Minors, and he warms up and they go through their batting order with him pitching full bore.

He's good.

Then I remember.

In Utah, they got this rule that in little league a pitcher can't pitch more than ten innings in any forty eight hour period. I wonder about whether they got that rule here. If they do, that means I can only pitch three innings against these guys.

And that means Jackie gets four innings, and from what I'm seeing, they're going to get about fifteen runs in those innings.

After while Stone shows up and walks over and sits down in the grass beside me.

"How's the hand," I ask?

"Fine, oh fine, just fine." He grins at me.

"Let me see."

It's red and a little puffy.

"You better soak that thing,"

"I did. It's fine."

"What's the name of our second baseman," I ask.

Stone scrooches up his face while he thinks. "Oh, yeah, Webb. He's played before."

We watch while the Blue Jays close down practice and the coach calls them together and talks to them and you can tell he's giving them the game plan for playing us.

I turn to Stone. "You guys got the forty eight hour rule on pitchers here?"

"What rule?"

I tell him.

Stone shrugs. "Don't know."

The Blue Jays throw their gear in the bag and start for the parking lot as Coach Stern pulls in, and the coaches say hello and they talk a minute, and Stern waves at us, and goes on over to the bench. Our other guys are arriving as Stone and I get up and drift over to the diamond.

Coach calls us all to the bench and looks at notes on his clip-board.

"We get the Blue Jays tomorrow night and they're good. And, we got to remember, the rule is a pitcher can only pitch ten innings in any forty eight hour time period, so we'll have to use two pitchers tomorrow night. I got to do some thinking about how we'll work it. For right now, Coach Briggs'll take some of you and I'll take the rest, and we're going to do some drills. Okay, let's go."

It's all over with the Blue Jays. Jackie'll pitch the first four innings and they'll get a ton of runs, and I'll get the last three and there's no chance we'll catch them.

Briggs knocks flies to us in the outfield while coach runs infield drills, and then he calls us in for batting practice and he really bears down on bunting, and he spends a lot of time with Bernie because Bernie can't get the hang of sliding your hand up the bat barrel and at the same time turning and planting your feet to square with the pitcher.

Then coach says, "Okay, we run bases against the clock," and here's where I get a heavy duty surprise.

Bernie takes his turn, and he stands on home plate and the coach says "go" and he starts for first and he looks like a giraffe. It takes about ten steps before he gets all those tinker toys in sinc, and then his running takes on sort of a really weird rhythm, and he rounds first and he's moving pretty good, and he rounds second and he's still gaining a little speed, and he crosses home plate and the coach's stop watch is on sixteen.

I can't believe it! He's the fastest on the team! I run it in about eighteen, and most of us are higher than that, except Stone. He's second fastest at seventeen. Coach says something about it and Bernie don't crack a smile. Rich guys don't smile.

We finish about seven o'clock and coach tells us to be on time for the game, and we gather up the equipment and Webb gets one of the big canvas equipment bags and Randy gets the other, and I move in to work with Webb.

"Is Minors good?," I ask while he holds one bag and I toss in green stained practice balls. I know Minors is good because I watched him, but see, you gotta know your own guys, whether they're tigers or pussycats and I don't know Webb hardly at all.

"Yeah. Good."

"We in trouble?"

He doesn't say anything, but I glance at his eyes and I can see it. He's afraid. If the rest of the team is, we just as well forfeit the game and stay home.

I bicycle home and walk in the door quiet and Mom gets a warm supper from the oven and I eat. The Geezer's there, but he doesn't say anything, and I go to my room, and I lay on my back in the dark, staring at the ceiling for a long time.

I'm up early and finish trimming the shrubs along the cinderblock wall of the back yard, and an hour before game time I put on my uniform and the Geezer comes home and the family eats supper, except me. I drink a glass of orange juice and that's all because it's hard to play with stuff in your stomach.

The Geezer drives me down to the park and I walk stocking footed to the bench and put on my cleats while the other guys get there. Coach comes and we carry the equipment bags over and we hang the bats in the chain link, and he tells us to sit on the bench.

"Okay, here's how we're going to handle this."

He's smiling one of those psychology smiles and I look at my shoes and shake my head because I know how we're going to handle it. Jackie takes the first four innings and it won't make any difference what I do in the last three.

"Lineup is just like last game. Joe, you start on the mound."

I nearly choke. This is nuts. I mean, everyone knows Jackie

was going to take the first four innings while we pray they don't get so far ahead we can't catch them in the last three.

The infield trots out for our ten minute warmup and Ned and I go over to get my arm loosened up. They're home team so we bat first. While they're warming up, coach calls Bernie over and they're close enough that I can hear.

"First time up, you're going to bunt."

Bernie's eyes get big. "Bunt, coach? Like in . . . bunt?"

I think I've heard wrong. Bernie's our cleanup batter. He's supposed to hit.

"Like in bunt, Bernie."

Bernie stands full up and bobs his head once like he can't believe it and says, "Bunt. Like in . . bunt."

"Batter up," says the blue and Ned goes out to the plate.

He gets a pretty good rap but is thrown out at first in a close play.

Randy walks to the box. Randy is a real nice kid with those soft brown eyes and doesn't say much. Sort of tall and dark with a lean look and you don't notice him because he's so quiet but after a while, if you watch, you see he's got the makings of a pretty good all around player.

Randy pops one in the hole over second and gets to first base.

Chin is next. He closes his dictionary and jams it in his hip pocket and trots to the plate.

On a real close call, he gets walked.

Bernie comes up with these two guys on first and second.

The Blue Jay infield moves back and the outfield trots thirty feet back.

Those guys know the one thing you don't want in baseball is to let a ball get behind you so you have to chase it. If you do, you're running the wrong direction, and when you get it you got to stop and turn and take your two steps to get leverage, and while you're doing all that the runner gets an extra base. So don't let the ball get behind you.

Bernie takes the first pitch, a called strike and I can see him thinking bunt and he's really struggling.

The second pitch, he tries to slip his right hand up the bat barrel and crouch and move his feet at the same time and he doesn't quite get it all put together, but he makes contact and lays down a real lousy bunt that dribbles out half ways between the mound and first base.

Easy, sure, certain, automatic out, right?

Wrong.

The idea Bernie would bunt, and the loony way he made the moves shocks Minors and the infield and they just stand there for at least two seconds like they seen a ghost, while Bernie's chugging down to first, and the ball stops before Minors wakes up and charges it. He barehands it and cocks to throw and he loses it and grabs for it and makes this real crappy off balance throw that misses first base by ten feet and the ball rolls out twenty feet past the big tree out behind first.

Briggs is coaching first and he windmills Bernie on to second and Bernie don't stop chugging and their first baseman gets the ball and turns and fires hard for second, and I swear, the sight of all Bernie's tinker toys coming like a herd of giraffe's scares their second baseman so bad he freezes and he can't hang onto the throw from first.

Bernie pulls up safe at second and Randy and Chin have both crossed the plate, and Bernie turns to our bench and he looks like, just thought you guys would like to see how it's done.

We look at him and I yell "Way to go," but nobody else yells much of anything.

Two runs.

Denny strikes out and after him Webb hits a slow roller down the third base line and their third baseman fields it easy, hesitates to hold Bernie on second, and Webb beats the throw to first.

I'm up. Bernie's on second, Webb's on first.

I take the first pitch, a called ball and the second one, a called strike.

Eyes down - watch the ball for contact - you win games on singles. It's going through my brain like a recording.

I watch the ball leave Minors fingers and I watch it right on to the plate and it's a fast ball and I just come around to meet it and I hear tink and it's just an average, everyday single over the second baseman's head.

At the crack of the bat Bernie windmills right on around third and slides under the throw, and Webb rounds second and looks at third and coach stops him and he goes back to second. I'm on first, Webb's on second, Bernie's scored.

This is all backwards! We've got three runs! They're supposed to have three runs in the first, not us.

Jackie hits a dribbler and is thrown out at first and the top of the first is in the books.

We trot to the dugout and things are quiet while we all try to figure out how we got three runs, and coach says, "Joe and Ned, come here for a minute."

We huddle.

"Joe, strike out the first man and walk the next two."

My head jerks and I blurt out, "Walk two guys?"

"Walk them."

"You mean a pitch out? I seen these guys today and I can take 'em."

"No, throw a strike or two, but walk them, and make it look like you didn't mean to do it."

Ned looks at coach, and then me, and his upper lip curls like he's got diarrhea.

"When do we get the last two outs?," I ask him.

"Their fourth and fifth batters."

"You're saying first one goes down, second two I walk, next two go down?"

"You got it." He's smiling. "You'll do fine."

I look at Ned and he shrugs and we trot to our positions.

I throw my warmups and the blue yells, "Batter up" and their first batter comes to the plate.

One fast ball and one curve ball and another fast ball later he's out and he walks back to the dugout kicking dirt all the way.

Second man comes up. Five pitches later he's on first by a walk.

Every guy on their bench is on his feet, giving me fits. "Open a new can of pitchers - this one's gone."

I feel absolutely world class crummy.

Next batter comes up, six pitches, and he's going to first while the other guy trots over to second.

Their bench is going bonkers. They're jumping around, yelling, and I can hear noise from the bleachers. See, the

47

people in the bleachers are mostly the family and friends of the players, which means half of them yell for one team, half for the other. The Blue Jay half is tearing up the place really bad.

The next two guys, batters number four and five, are their cleanup hitters, and I mean, those two guys are barbarians. I look the first one in the eye because usually a batter will look cocky or scared or ferocious or ho hum or what's on for supper, and if you can learn to read it you can sort of tell how he's going to swing.

This first guy's Atilla the Hun! I mean, he's standing there and he's not making a sound but I hear it like he's on a loud speaker - one fastball down the middle - just one - you won't ever find it because it'll be down south of Foothill.

Ned signs a curve and I shake it off and Ned signs a fastball and I wind up and deliver.

Ned's mouth forms that little "ooooo" when it whacks into his mitt and this guy never gets his bat off his shoulder and the crowd goes quiet.

He spits between his teeth like tough guys do and once again faces me and his jaw's clenched and his lower lip's stuck out a mile, and there's murder written all over his face.

Ned signs curve and I shake it off and crank up another fastball.

"Steerike" bellows the blue.

I mean, this guy nearly starts after me with the bat! He settles down and his lip is back in place when he plants his feet, and his face is the picture of determination.

Ned signs fastball and I shake it off and crank up a curve.
I throw it nearly right at the guy's head and he pulls his head in like a turtle and spins away and the ball curves back and down and crosses the corner of the plate.

"Steerike" hollers the blue and jerks his thumb up and the guy is out.

He stands there, and he starts to hop up and down, and his coach yells at him and he don't listen, and the blue calls, "Next batter," and his coach has to come grab him.

Number five batter comes up, and he's supposed to be their second clean up man.

I take the sign and the first two pitches are fastballs, one a called strike, the other swung on and missed.

I own this bozo. Ned signs sinker, and I don't change my face expression. It looks a lot like a fastball until it gets about ten feet from the plate and this guy is swinging from his heels and when it's about five feet from the plate the bottom falls out and it drops like a rock and he tries to correct and can't, and he misses it eight inches and Ned has his glove in the dirt when he catches it.

"Steerike" calls the blue and the bottom of the first is in the books, and we're leading, three - zip.

The Reds half of the bleachers is on their feet yelling, and the Blue Jay bench is sitting down, heads forward, faces white. We trot to the bench and watch the Blue Jays take the field, and I can see something's wrong. I mean, there's no talk, no swagger, no spitting, - they just go out there like sleepwalkers for their warmup.

Second inning we score one more run, and we're gathering up our mitts to go back out when coach calls a huddle.

"Jackie, you take the mound, Joe, center field, Bernie, left field."

This guy's lost it!

He tells the blue and then the other coach, and the other coach stands there with his mouth open and then shrugs, and when Jackie trots out to the mound the Blue Jays go dead silent. They sit down on the bench and they look like they're two clicks off plumb.

The bottom of their lineup comes to bat, their weakest batters. Jackie puts one man on by a walk but the next two are thrown out on infield grounders, and the fourth guy bangs a pop fly to Webb, and they're through in the second.

Still four to zip, our favor.

In the next three innings I get one more hit and we leave four or five guys on base but we don't score. Coach makes Bernie bunt two more times, and he's out both times. The Blue Jays are starting to get their bearings again, and I can tell it's just a matter of time before they knock the ball all over the field.

Jackie has learned that if a pitcher can't throw hard he has to throw smart, and Jackie knows he can't throw very hard. So he mixes things up, like a fast ball and a curve and then a slider, or anything to keep them guessing. He knows they're going to get hits, so all he can do is try to control it so it goes to someone in the infield, or a fly to the outfield. That's when a pitcher depends on his team for backup.

They get one run in the fourth.

In the fifth, as they're starting to get their balance again, the wheels start to come off our wagon.

Randy boots a grounder and the guy pulls up at first. Stone takes a grounder and thinks he can get the guy sliding at second but he throws too low and Webb can't dig it out of the dirt and it gets past him and both runners advance, second and third, while he's running it down.

Their next batter sacrifices with a long fly to left and Bernie catches it but the runner on third scores and the runner on second advances to third.

Next guy lays down a good bunt and runs right over it on the way to first and Jackie can't pick it up until it's too late and the runner on third scores.

Their next man smacks a bouncing double to me and I field it and throw to the cut off man because its too late to do anything about the run crossing the plate.

A stocky little guy steps into the batters box, and grounds out, and their next hitter knocks a double to right field and another run scores, and the next batter flies out.

The fifth inning is over, but they've scored five, and they're over on their bench talking and they've got a strong rally going and they know they're going to cream us the last two innings.

The problem is, we know it too.

Then coach calls us over, and he lays one on us that stops me cold.

"Joe, back to the mound, Bernie back to center, Jackie back to right."

I stand there for a minute while my brain searches to explain the really bizarre way coach has handled this game, and suddenly it comes to me.

The Blue Jays knew they were going to get Jackie the first four innings and they were all ready to kill him.

They got me instead and you know, that tipped them off balance just a little tiny bit. Not bad.

Then, I got the first guy, walked two, then nailed the next two guys, and they were finished in the first.

I mean, now they're way off balance. The reason is, we've gone through their murderers row in the first inning, without a single run. Their best hitters, the first five, are dead. So, then coach sticks Jackie in just as the next inning begins, and they don't expect that either, and now they're wondering just what's going on. Jackie faces their last four hitters - their worst - and if Jackie can put them down one, two, three, then he starts the fourth inning with their ninth batter. If he can get that one, he's only got part of the fourth inning and all of the fifth to worry about, because coach can put me back in for the sixth and seventh.

All told, the Blue Jays didn't really get their balance until the fifth inning and they really jumped on us, and they come out in the sixth ready to nuke Jackie again.

But they don't get Jackie! They're looking at me again, and now they're off balance so bad they couldn't hit the backstop with their mitt.

Now, that's coaching baseball!

I glance at coach and he's standing there like what's the big deal, and I start to trot out to the mound when I hear this big voice boom out.

"Hold on there."

The Blue Jay coach shambles out from behind their chain link and his chin's shoved out like a bulldog.

"Stern, that aint legal."

Both umpires walk over for the showdown.

"You can't split the innings for a pitcher. If Russell pitched one inning at the first of the game you can't call him back later to pitch again."

Coach Stern smiles and says, "Oh? Got your rule book?"

Both coaches and both blues pull out their rule books and Stern says, "Look right here, on page . . . 9 paragraph 8a."

Stern's face is real pleasant. "Re-entry rule. A pitcher can not re-enter the game as a pitcher if he has left the field of play."

The other coach - name's Condi - gets a real smarty look on his face and says, "Right there. Like I said. Russell's through

51

on the mound."

Stern shakes his head. "He never left the field of play."

Condi's head jerks forward and the senior blue reads it again, and Condi says, "Wait a minute. He left the mound. That's what the rule's talking about."

Stern smiles. "He didn't leave the field of play. That's what the rule says."

Condi blusters, "But that's how we've always done it."

Stern turns to the senior blue. "What's your call?"

The blue shakes his head. "The field of play is the field of play. It don't say mound. Russell can pitch."

Wow! The Blue Jays look like they just saw Frankenstein. You can just see the steam drain out of them, like a leaky boiler.

Sixth inning, three up, three down.

And that brings us to the seventh.

We're down one run, five to four, and we're at bat first. We got to manufacture two runs somehow.

Ned grounds out to first.

Randy comes up.

"Tink." He beats out a long throw from their short stop and is safe at first.

Chin shoves that book back in his pocket and comes to the plate. Minors tries to strike him out and misses on a three and two, and walks him to first and now we got Randy on second.

Bernie is next. Coach calls a huddle.

"Bernie," he says, "I'm going to give you the bunt sign again, loud and clear, when you're in the batters box. When I do, square to bunt but don't bunt. Then on the second pitch I'm going to sign bunt again. This time ignore it. Hit away. You understand?"

Bernie nods. "Yessir I hear you."

He takes his lanky stance in the batters box and coach steps to the third base coaching box and turns to Bernie and gives him the bunt sign and everybody in the ballpark sees it. Bernie nods his head.

Minors is suspicious and coach Condi's so nervous he can't stand still, but they're both remembering Bernie's bunt in the first inning. Minors watches Condi while Condi paces and the blue finally yells, "Play ball or forfeit," and Condi's got no choice.

He gives the signal. Everybody in for a bunt.

The Blue Jay infield moves forward four steps and the out-field moves in ten.

Minors delivers and Bernie drops into bunt position but doesn't bunt and takes a called strike. High, but it was a strike. All eyes on both teams go back to Stern. He gives the same sign and Bernie nods and Condi signals his team to stay up for a bunt.

Minors cranks up and delivers a nice, straight, right down the groove fast ball, perfect for a bunt, and every Blue Jay is mov-ing forward to pick it up in time for a double play.

But Bernie doesn't square up for a bunt. He takes a full stride and swings with all he's got.

"Tank."

It's a bullet and it screams past third twenty feet high and it's fair when it passes the base but it's hooking left real hard, and for just a second everyone at Griffith Park freezes to watch it settle.

Our whole team is on its feet, leaning forward, mouths open and we're staring like we're hypnotized.

I think we're watching slow motion. It takes about a year for that thing to settle and just before it kisses down I know it's going to be one inch foul but then it hits and we all see a puff of chalk as it hits the base line!

Fair!

Randy and Chin both cross the plate and Bernie pulls up at second, and we're up six to five, and we're over there and for the first time in the whole season, one of our guys hollers, "Way to go!"

I look at Bernie and he's so surprised he freezes and his eyes are popping and his jaw's on his belt buckle for a second before he snaps it shut and looks rich.

Our next guy strikes out, but we're up six to five going into the bottom of the seventh.

I trot to the mound and throw a couple and nod to the blue and he bawls "Batter up" and their first guy comes to the plate.

I look at his eyes and they're glassy and he's sweating.

I know he's expecting a fastball and I shake off Ned's sign and then he signs sinker, and I throw this humongous sinker that drops a foot. This guy misses eight inches and his sweaty hands slip on the bat and he throws it clear over the Blue Jay bench, and right then I know those guys are finished. Two more pitches and this guy's out.

The next batter gets a tiny piece of a fastball and it dribbles back to me and I underhand to Chin and he's out.

Their last batter comes up and his eyes are almost pleading. Please. Please. A hit.

The guy goes white watching a fastball, and then he misses a curveball, and then I move him back with a hard one inside, and then I fire this fastball over the outside corner, and he lunges so hard when he swings that he falls to his knees, and I feel sorry for him.

"Steerrike" calls the blue, and this guy gets up and it's over.

We beat them! We beat the Blue Jays. There's no sense to it, but it's in the book, and we won it!

The bleachers are going insane.

I walk over to Randy. "Come on."

He looks startled but he follows me and I walk straight to Bernie. "Man, that was some kind of hit. I mean, you won that one."

For a split second Bernie's mouth drops open and he can't say anything. I jab Randy in the ribs and he grunts and I give him a look that would kill a hippo and he looks at Bernie and he says, "Yeah. That was great."

Bernie closes his mouth and he sort of mumbles something like, "Right. Yeah. Big deal."

He turns and walks away and I'm thinking, how much money does it take to make a guy that way?

Mendoza yells, "Way to pitch," and I turn and wink and he grins, but nobody else yells anything.

Out of the corner of my eye I see Chin, and I turn to glance, and he's standing there with that book in his hand, and that stone face of his, but I can see he's starting to understand.

We walk through the line to exchange high fives with the Blue Jays and they won't look us in the eye. Their coach gives Stern's hand one pump and turns back to start loading equipment.

Coach huddles us. "Good job. Next practice is Saturday. Be

here."

The Geezer's waiting at the car and I walk over there with my cleats clicking on the asphalt.

On the ride home he whistles for a minute and then says, "Pretty good game, huh?"

"Yeah. Good."

"You got a couple hits."

I shrug and don't say anything.

"Smart coach."

"Lucky," I say.

"Yeah, and I think he'll probably get lucky a couple more times this season."

MOM WINS BIG

"EARL NEEDS HELP WITH A new roof. Pays five bucks an hour. I told him you'll call this morning."

He did it again! He never says anything like, "Joe, Earl needs help on his roof. What do you think? Can you help him?" He just decides I'm going to help and tells me to call. It's always, I've done the thinking because you're a dumb kid and I've decided what you're going to do, and just be quiet and don't talk back and go do it.

"And spend some time with the batting tee."

Why couldn't he say, "Joe, how's the batting? Do you think more time with the tee would help?"

I mean, I'm not dumb. I got some good ideas. I got some smarts. He's forgotten what it does to a guy inside to be put down and told everything he has to do like he's a retard. He doesn't know I'd lay down and die if he once, just once, walked over and said, "Joe, that was great. You did good."

I jam some scrambled eggs into my mouth so I won't have to answer him and reach for my glass of orange juice.

The Geezer gets up from the breakfast table and takes his dirty dishes to the sink and turns to Mom.

"I'll be in Sacramento for the next game."

"Be careful," she say. "I'll go to the game."

I cringe at the thought. I finish breakfast while he walks out the door, and force my thoughts to the roof job at Earl's, and then the batting tee.

Earl's a good old guy that flew P-38 fighters in World War II, and I finish breakfast and get his number and call.

"Got a lot of gravel to get off the roof," Earl says, "and tar to put down. It'll take a couple weeks. Pays five bucks an hour. Starts today."

"I got ball practice and games."

"Time off for those."

We make a deal and I sigh and head for my room. I'll have to wear old beat up clothes because this roof job is going to get messy.

At three o'clock I lay down this monster sized, heavy bristled broom and look at the mountain of gravel I've shoveled to one side of the roof, and then swept up, and I'm sweated out and my hands feel puffy inside the heavy gloves. It had to be one hundred twenty degrees on that roof.

Earl smiles and nods and I head for home. I shower and change into my practice clothes and Mom puts a baloney sandwich and milk on the table and I gulp it down and head out for my bike. I get to Griffith early, to watch whoever's practicing, and after a few minutes I figure out it's the Cardinals. That's the team we play next. I watch for a while out by the trees and pretty soon Webb walks up and sits down.

"They any good?"

I shrug. "Don't know. Only been here ten minutes."

We sit there quiet for a minute and then I ask, "You ever played for coach before?"

"Nope."

"Mendoza ever played before?"

"Nope. Been on a team, but never played."

"Why does he come out?"

Webb shrugs. "Seems like nobody wants him on anything, even at school. If you come out for Pony league, they got to put you on a team, and he just wants to belong to something, I guess. Loves baseball."

"Where does he live?"

"Out by the gravel pit."

"Family?"

Webb grins like I said something funny. "Yeah."

"What does Bernie's dad do?"

"Brain doctor."

"Ever come out to watch Bernie?"

"Nope. Too busy."

A car door slams behind us and the Stott brothers walk over and plop down.

"What's up," Randy says.

I shrug. "Nothing."

Pretty soon Chin shows up and walks over and leans against the tree and doesn't say anything. We look at him and don't say anything either.

Coach drives up and we help with the bags, and the Cardinals shut down their practice and we go over to start ours, and coach gets us gathered at home plate.

"Briggs will take practice while I talk to you, one at a time. Webb, come with me."

I walk to the infield with the team while coach sits down on the bench with Webb. Briggs knocks us fungoes, and while we're working the infield I watch our guys. Randy's quiet and has those big brown eyes but he moves pretty good. Denny, his brother, is blonde and comes on pretty strong, and he's built heavier. Chin's shorter, and he's starting to look like he knows what's going on. Stone's all over third base like a mosquito. And then there's Mendoza.

"Joe, next."

Webb trots out to my place and I go sit on the bench by coach. "Joe, you're doing good. Just a couple of things. First, do you like it here in California?"

"Yeah. It's okay."

"Good. You got a good arm. How do you feel at batting?"

"I work at it."

"Your average is .307. Satisfied with that?"

"Well, no, not really."

"You practice at home?"

"Yeah."

"Okay. Keep practicing. Keep your head down, eye on the

ball until you make contact. Don't try to hit it hard, just meet it. Games are won with singles and doubles, not long balls. Okay?"

He's talked with the Geezer! Conspiracy!

"Yeah. Okay."

"Let's give it a try."

We spend a few minutes with the batting tee and he smiles like he's satisfied, and calls Stone. Practice ends and I'm heading for my bike, watching, and the black aircraft carrier pulls up for Chin.

"Who drives that thing," I ask Jackie.

"A chauffeur or somethin'."

"What does Chin's dad do?"

Jackie thinks. "Clothes business, Taiwan maybe."

"Where does Chin live?"

"Up on Laurel."

"Who with?"

"Housekeeper and sometimes his mom and about once a year his dad shows up."

I slip my mitt onto my bike handlebars and start for home while the cars pull out, and I watch the Cadillacs and the Lincoln limo, and then I watch Mendoza peddle away on that freaky bicycle of his with his beat up old mitt on the handlebar.

Next morning's clear, and by ten I'm on top of Earl's roof, dirty and sweating. I lay in the shade and eat a sandwich Mom sent for lunch, then back up on the roof until three.

Earl says, "Good luck" when I come down. I shower and drink a lot of orange juice and lay down until a little after four, and then I get up and start getting dressed. I carry my cleats to the kitchen to keep from marking Mom's floors, and I stop for another half glass of orange juice.

"Ready," she asks.

"Yeah." I put the glass down, and start getting braced for what Mom does at baseball games.

The problem is, she doesn't know anything about baseball. She knows the idea is to throw a ball across a piece of rubber and someone is supposed to hit it with a stick and run around three bases. So far as she knows, which direction they run doesn't matter. When something happens more than that, she's got about two or three things she yells to cover up what she doesn't know.

"Kill the ump!"

"We wuz robbed!"

"You blind or somethin'?"

That's her whole book on baseball. If that was the entire problem maybe I could handle it by figuring out a way to have her stay away from my games, but there's more.

Mom thinks she's got this life calling from Heaven to do everything with us kids. I'll bet she's seen five hundred basketball and volleyball games, and I wouldn't know how many church things, and baked maybe ten tons of cakes and cookies for fund raisers for our teams, and been chaperone for at least one hundred dances and overnighters, all for us eight kids.

Let me give a for instance.

Here I am, six feet tall, at a summer camp with a lot of guys, and here comes Mom driving the Chevy into camp with six dozen cinnamon rolls she volunteered to bake. She won't just put them on the nearest table and go on back home. She sits them down and comes looking for me.

"Hungry? Sleeping well? Changing your socks?"

The other guys stand there trying to be respectful, and they stare at the ground and shift from one foot to the other.

"Washing your hands before every meal? Combing your hair?"

My stomach cramps. "Yeah, Mom, I'm fine. Thanks for the cinnamon rolls. The guys will love you. The sun goes down early up here so maybe you better start home."

She doesn't blink. "Cold at night? Drinking four glasses of water each day? Need some clean shorts?"

And it goes on and on and on.

Mom parks at Griffith at four thirty and I walk to the bench and start with my cleats while she takes a seat on the third row up in the bleachers, right behind the plate. Our guys drift in and the Cardinals start to show, and by four forty we're going through our ten minute warmup. We sit while they warm up, and they don't look scary at all. They're not supposed to be a threat, but baseball is a crazy game. You never know. You take them all serious or sooner or later you get burned.

Coach starts Jackie on the mound, which is what I figured, because our next game's in two days, and we play the Orioles. They're already tagged as the heavy team in the league, and I know the coach is worried. He wants me ready for that game.

He starts me in center field, Bernie in left, Denny in right. Stone on third, Randy at short, Webb on second, Chin on first, and Ned catching.

Mom's right in the middle of the crowd in the bleachers. See, mom's a pretty classy, real proper looking lady when she goes out in public. I mean, she's 56 just like dad, but she doesn't have a gray hair in her head, and she's tall and she looks real stately when she's sitting quiet. It just knocks people cold in a baseball game when this proper lady comes out with this truck driver's voice, "Kill The Ump!"

I mumble a prayer, "Let this game go smooth. Help Mom to keep her mouth shut."

We're home team, the blue yells "Batter up," we trot out to our positions, and Jackie takes the first signal from Ned.

We hold them to one run in the first inning, and trot to the bench for our first at bat. With two out and the bases loaded I walk to the plate and the pitcher throws two balls and two strikes.

Head down, watch the ball, just swing to meet it.

"Tink." Blooper single just over first baseman's head and we score one run.

Next batter grounds out to third and first inning is history.

Second inning, their pitcher comes up. His name's Ken Zimmer and besides pitching, he's one of their heavy hitters.

Coach signs a pitchout, and Ned steps five feet from the plate, and Jackie just lobs him the ball, real easy, you know, a regular old every day pitch out where you walk the guy on purpose because you're afraid he'll cream the ball.

"Ball," calls the ump, and Mom hears this, and she sees what's going on, and she starts to fuss and I look up at her.

Coach signals again, and Ned leaves the box and Jackie lobs the second ball in the pitch out.

"Ball," shouts the ump.

Mom suddenly understands the ump is calling balls on our pitcher, and she lunges to her feet and her voice shakes the backstop.

"What's the matter, you blind?"

Every eye in Griffith field swings around to look at who it is yelling so stupid, and they can't believe it's this proper looking grand mother type lady in the bleachers with the fog horn voice.

I turn around in center field and study the backstop down at the south end of Griffith Park.

Jackie delivers the next ball on the pitch out.

"Ball three" says the ump.

"KILL THE UMP" shouts mom.

I hear little titters of laughter clear out in center field.

Jackie looks scared and stares at the coach. Stern gives him the pitch out sign again and Ned is standing five steps towards first base, and Jackie delivers the last ball.

"Ball four," shouts the ump.

"YER MOTHER WEARS ARMY BOOTS" roars mom.

She's learned a new one.

Everybody in the bleachers starts to laugh and then they all stand up and break out in applause.

Mom stands and bows like she's on a stage. Real proud, like she's done her duty, and she's smiling at everyone.

When the inning is over I trot to the dugout and sit down quick and don't look back.

"Joe." It's her voice behind me and I act like I didn't hear.

"Joe!" This time it's loud and everything goes quiet and I have to turn and look.

"Joe, tell the umpire to be fair."

I hear people slapping their hands over their mouths and I turn back and scrooch my head down a little and play like I got something in my eye.

"Joe, he isn't being fair. Tell him."

The guys all lean forward and look at me, and finally Stone says, "Joe, you run right over there and tell the blue to cut that out."

The guys all grin and the smart remarks continue.

"Joe, don't let that big bad man do those naughty things."

"Joe, go over and tell him to be nice."

Everybody in the park starts to laugh, and then the remarks

come from the bleachers like an avalanche. Mom thinks she's started a real neat thing, to support her kid.

I finally look around at Mom and give her a sit down sign, and she sits down and things quiet. About a year later the blue quits laughing and slaps his mask on and shouts, "Play ball."

Jackie gets into trouble fast. We get one out, then they get a double and a single and Jackie walks a man. Bases are full, with only one out.

Jackie starts to sweat and walks the next guy, and that forces the guy on third home, free. So the guy starts to trot from third to towards home real slow, with a real insulting grin to let us know how crummy our team is, walking him home.

Mom sees him trotting down towards home plate and suddenly she gasps. This guy's on the Cardinals team and he's heading towards home plate and if he crosses home plate, they get another run. That's all she understands!

Then she sees Ned standing there on the plate watching the guy who got walked trot towards first while Ned smacks the ball into his mitt, disgusted.

And Mom leaps up, absolutely convinced Ned doesn't see the guy trotting in from third!

We get this fog horn blast, "Little boy, little boy!"

Ned jumps about a foot and turns and looks and then points to himself. He wants to know if she means him.

"Yes, you. There is a man running towards home plate from over there." She points because she doesn't know first from third. She only knows when anyone crosses home plate they add one point.

Ned nods that he knows it.

The guy is just ten feet from the plate, trotting slow.

Mom panics. "DO SOMETHING." The backstop trembles.

Ned looks at coach, scared, and coach hunches his shoulders and laughs.

Ned looks at the ball like it's a rattlesnake and throws it back to Jackie.

Mom's pointing at the guy coming in from third, and she's jumping up and down, and he crosses the plate, and mom bellows, "WE WUZ ROBBED."

The place falls to pieces. I mean, people are nearly rolling out of the bleachers. The other coach is in hysterics. The players are on both teams are flopping around on the ground. The blues are leaning against the backstop to stay on their feet.

I bend over and tie my shoes. I pull up my socks. I adjust my stirrups. I tighten my belt. I dig something out of my eye. I stare at the south field. I scratch my back side. I glance at seagulls flying over.

Finally the blue hollers "Batter up" and the game continues, while the remarks from the bleachers go on for the next four innings, non-stop.

But the all time show stopper comes in the bottom of the seventh when we're batting.

See, everybody at Griffith got so caught up in the comedy that we about forgot to play ball, and we're down to our last at bat and the score's tied! We should be four runs ahead, but we've just been goofing, and there we are, tied.

Then Webb hits a screamer out past center fielder and figures he can stretch a sure triple to a home run. He rounds third and the coach has both hands up to hold him on third but Webb either doesn't see or thinks he's being waved home and he rounds third base kicking dirt at every stride. Their relay man on second takes the incoming throw and turns and throws to the plate and here comes Webb, sliding under the throw.

It's close. Calling Webb safe or out depends on where you're standing. Our bench saw him safe and theirs saw him out.

The blues got hand signals for most everything. Strike is signaled with the right hand, balls left. If a guy's safe, the blue signals with arms thrown wide, palms down. If the guy's out, the right hand jerks up. And when they give the hand signal, they usually make a voice call with it.

So Webb hooks the plate with his toe and the catcher puts the mitt on him, and the blue at the plate takes half a second to be sure, and then he throws his arms out, palms down. Webb's safe.

But he doesn't make his usual voice call.

What he does, he slowly straightens, and he removes his face mask, and he turns around and faces the bleachers. He puts his mask over his heart like he's saluting the flag, and looks until he locates Mom, and he stands there like a soldier, heels together, and the place goes quiet.

"Madame, what say you? Safe or out?"

Now the place is dead silent. We can hear the bees buzzing among the dandelions. Everybody in the park is holding their breath waiting.

Mother clears her throat and smiles like she does this every day, and she says, "I think that nice young man was safe."

"SAFE," bawls the blue and the game's over. We won in the bottom of the seventh on mom's call.

You can hear the pandemonium for two blocks and it goes on for minutes. People gather around Mom and she gabs and chats with them like she's known them forever. Coach goes over and takes off his hat and introduces himself and they shake hands and talk for a few minutes and I see Mom nod her head to something he says before he comes back.

Coach waves us in. I'm staring off into the parking lot like I'm looking for someone and he finally calls me by name.

"Gather round," Coach says. "Next game is the Orioles in two more days. Practice tomorrow. Five oclock. Be here."

That sobers us. The Orioles are the heavy team, at least for the first half of the season. It's game number four of our six game half season.

I turn to help with the equipment and coach calls me aside.

"Mendoza needs help. What do you say?"

I look at him, puzzled. "Now?"

"No, extra."

"Help at what?"

"All of it."

I shrug. "Sure." While I'm jamming balls and bats into the bag, I look around for him, but he's gone.

Mom drives the Chevy home and chatters the whole way. I don't even try to tell her what she's done. As we park in the driveway she lays the ultimate on me.

"Oh, Joe, that nice coach asked me if I would be the official team mother. I told him I would. I'm supposed to call other mothers and get them organized. I have to bring some cinnamon rolls for the team after the next game."

I tip my head back and close my eyes and they roll up into my head. If I quit the team, will they return half my fifty bucks? I let Mom get out and go into the house until I recover.

7

NOSE TO NOSE, TOE TO TOE

MENDOZA. PRACTICE HIM EXTRA. Coach's orders are on my mind when my eyes open next morning.

I sweat on Earl's roof until two o'clock and we stop for the day while he cuts up more cold tar and tosses it in the cooker for tomorrow, and I head for home. I clean up and eat spaghetti and Mom makes a call to find out where the gravel pit is, and I peddle east on Baseline.

The houses end and vacant lots and weeds take over, and I cross Monte Vista, and there's a barbed wire fence, and a little further, there's the gravel pit. It's a humungous hole in the ground with a crane and a big bulldozer and water in ponds at the bottom, and they look small they're so far down and far away. On the far rim of the crater is a house, and I peddle on to the open gate in the barbed wire fence and turn in on a rutted gravel road.

There's no grass or trees. All I can see is a sort of beat up shack and an old junked out Studebaker without tires, and a rattle trap flat bed truck, and a whole bunch of little kids that look just like Mendoza. I stop in the yard and a girl about ten runs over to me.

"Mendoza here?," I ask.

"Papa?"

"No. Baseball."

"Felipe." She runs yelling and Mendoza comes out from behind a sagging shed. He has a broken handled wrench in his hand and three little barefooted kids right behind him, hanging onto his leg and peeking around. He stops to look at me and his eyes drop and I can see he wishes I hadn't come.

"Fixin' my bike," he says.

"Wanna come down to the field? Maybe throw a few?"

He freezes. Just absolutely freezes. "Baseballs? Me?"

I shrug. "Yeah."

He looks at the flock of barefoot kids, some without shirts, and he says, "Can't. Mama won't be back for a while."

"When?"

"I dunno. Maybe four."

"Come on over then."

I can see the doubt. "Sure."

Down in the pit, a long way off, the big diesel engine on the crane is roaring and belching smoke and I glance down as I peddle back to Baseline.

And I'm thinking, how many kids was there? Man, there musta been ten. I glance back and he's still standing there with that busted wrench in his hand and at least six little kids are standing there with him, watching me peddle back across Monte Vista, where the dirt road and the weeds and vacant lots end and the flowers and grass and stucco homes with palm trees and street lights begin.

He shows at Griffith a little after four and parks his junk heap bike near mine, and walks over. He puts his mitt on and the leather strings are broken and the webbing in the pocket flops at one corner, and the strap is fastened with a bent nail. I give him a head sign and he gets behind home plate and I start throwing easy to him from third base.

If I throw chest high and off to his left side where the mitt is, he can catch most of them. Anywhere else, more than half of them wind up in the dirt. Each time he moves as quick as two hundred twenty squatty pounds can, and he grunts to pick it up and throw it back, and he sprays his throws all over the place. I have to lunge to get a lot of them, and some I can't get at all.

"Hey," I call, "look right here." I point to my wishbone and he looks.

"Try to hit me right there."

He misses about four feet, but it's a lot better than the stuff he's been throwing.

"Good. Aim, see. Aim right there. Aim."

He nods and throws and misses about four feet again, but ten minutes later he's coming closer, and he's getting consistent. He starts to sweat and I can hear him wheeze when he throws.

"Wanna take a break?"

"Naw, we throw."

Twenty minutes later his shirt's soaked through and his long, black hair is plastered around his face, but he's tightened his pattern down to about three feet, and I'm watching his eyes and something's happening.

Stone shows up with Webb just before our five oclock practice and stops to watch, and they don't say anything. I catch Mendoza's last throw and I walk on in to home plate, and Mendoza stands there a minute and I think he wants to say something, but he doesn't, and then coach parks his pickup and the guys go to get the equipment bags.

Bernie and the rest get there, and Mendoza's all sweated out, and I see Bernie and Chin ask a couple questions and I think they're asking about why Mendoza looks boiled, but I don't hear what Stone and Webb tell him. Coach calls us together and we sit on the bench.

"We play the Orioles next, and they're the toughest team we'll play this half of the season."

He gives us the usual talk about do your job and keep under control, and then we run through the usual drills. We finish practice and Coach calls us back together.

"There's no tricky way to win this one. We just have to go out there and go straight at them. Don't be late for the game."

I bicycle home and it takes me half an hour going through cardboard boxes in the garage to find my old mitt, - the one I used from when I was five until I was twelve.

Every ballplayer knows you got to have a good mitt. Half of every game you play, you got a mitt on your hand, and if the mitt's a bummer, you haven't got a chance. It's got to be a

Wilson or a Rawlings with a big web and you got to work in a pocket just the way you want it. What you do, you get a soft-ball, and you shove it in the web and then you tie a lot of string tight around the mitt every night for a couple weeks, and slow-ly the pocket takes shape. And when you put the mitt on, you got to stick your fingers in the slots, all except your index fin-ger. That one you stick outside the slot, just because it looks so cool.

My mitt's a Wilson, full big league size. Stone's got one nearly as big, and when he's got it on it hangs clear past his knee. He looks sort of like a teeny gorilla out there, with his left hand nearly dragging in the dirt.

I sit down at the table before bed and get out my indelible pencil and wet it, and I draw heavy lines through my name on the mitt strap, and then I print MENDOZA on the back of the thumb. I work a little mink oil into it before I go to bed.

Next day I finish on Earl's roof by three, and by four I'm home and cleaned up and laying flat on my back on the the front room floor. I got my eyes closed and in my head I'm going over how I'm going to handle the game with the Oriole's. I figure it's going to be a pitching duel. They got this guy named Darrel Collins, and he's good. We're going to be lucky if we score three runs. More like one, or maybe we'll be shut out.

And they got some strong hitters. They're going to get a few hits.

Maybe this thing is going to cook down to who gets a break. Games between two teams that balance out equal are usually won or lost on some unexpected break that you never dreamed of. They just happen. You expect your heavy hitters to win for you, and they don't, so some other guy on the team that has never hit a homer in his life, smacks one clear out of sight in the bottom of the 7th and you win. Or some guy on their team does it, and you lose.

You never know. You make your plan and then you just pray the breaks fall your way.

By four twenty I'm at the field and when Mendoza gets there I toss him my old mitt with his name on it, and he stops and looks, and he sees his name, and he looks at me but doesn't say anything, and I shrug like, no big deal. He stands there and he slowly runs his fingers all over the mitt, and his eyes are bright, and he shoves his old mitt under our bench.

We warm up and then they warm up and I watch. I've scouted their last couple games, and my mouth is dry when the coach hands his lineup to the blue. The bleachers are filled when the blue shouts, "Batter up," and our game with the Orioles is under way.

They're home team so we bat first.

Ned picks out his thirty ounce Easton aluminum bat, and he takes a deep breath and balloons his cheeks when he lets it out, and he steps up to the plate. The bleachers are quiet, and the tension is there right from the first pitch.

The first three innings are tense, sweaty, nose to nose, toe to toe, brutal. We go down one, two, three, and they go down, one two, three.

Fourth inning, we mount our first threat. Ned knocks a dribbler down third base line and their third baseman fields it and misses the transfer of the ball from his mitt to his throwing hand and has to do it twice, and it costs him two extra steps and Ned beats the throw by half a step.

Randy steps to the plate, and he tries to check a swing but can't stop in time, and by pure accident taps the ball on the tip of the bat and lays down a perfect bunt, one foot inside the first base line, and beats out the throw. We got two on base.

Chin comes up, and cracks one to their shortstop and they pull a picturebook double play to third and second, and Ned and Randy are out. Our next batter strikes out and we're dead.

Next inning, they mount their first serious threat.

I strike out their first guy, and their second guy bangs an easy grounder to Webb at second and Webb fields it just like I figured it, but Webb underthrows Chin and Chin can't dig it out of the dirt and it gets past him, and their guy gets to second.

Their next batter hits one on the very top of the ball and drives it right into the dirt in front of the plate and it's spinning hard, and Ned rips off his mask and pounces and it spins away from his hand when he touches it, and he has to step to grab it, and he comes up cocked to throw to third, but the runner on second holds and now they got two guys on.

Their next batter steps up and Ned signs fastball and I put one a little high and outside, and this guy swings and hits it but it's far enough out that he can't get all his weight on it and it comes whistling past me towards first. I planned he'd hit it more towards second and Webb would field it for a double play.

I watch it come past and it's hot and looks like it's too high for Chin - it's going to clear his head by four feet. My heart sinks because if it gets past Chin they got one run sure, maybe two.

Both runners are off at the crack of the bat.

Chin jumps like a kangaroo and stretches everything he's got and snags the ball and it snowcones the top of his mitt as the runner on first comes past him on the way to second, and their coach screams "Get back". The kid turns to run back to first to tag up and Chin hits the ground and lunges and puts the ball on him, and then he spins and loads and fires to second and the runner that was on second has turned to tag up and Chin's throw smacks into Webb's mitt a microsecond before the runner's foot hits the bag and the base ump pumps his right arm and bawls, "Yer out!"

And just like that, bambambam, their threat's over. Chin pulled a triple play, assisted by Webb.

My shoulders slump with relief.

I hear one loud "Whoa" from Webb, and nothing from Chin. That face of his doesn't even change expression. He trots to the bench and sits down and he doesn't even look at the crowd in the bleachers, while they're yelling their heads off. He pulls that book out of his hip pocket and whips it open and concentrates.

I blow air as I trot to our bench and I sit by Chin and I say, "You saved us."

He turns a bunch of pages in his dictionary and then he reads to me in a twangy Pidgin-English, "Thank you, I have had enough to eat."

He knows something's wrong the minute he says it, and he whips the book open and turns the page and tracks with his finger while he silently mouths some words, and then he reads, "Thank you, I was very fortunate."

Then he looks at me sort of like, "Did I do it right that time?," and I smile and I nod.

"You done good."

He whips the book open again and gets lost looking for what I said.

Other than that, both benches are quiet. Everyone on both teams knows we're locked in a war and the first guy that blinks is going to lose.

Sixth inning, we bat.

Chin takes his stance and I look at Collins and I know exactly what he's going to do, and don't ask me how.

He dusts Chin off with a fast ball high and inside and that makes Chin just a little edgy.

Next pitch is a fast ball, belt high where Chin likes it but it's on the outside edge of the plate, but Chin can't resist. He takes his cut but makes contact too far out on the bat to get the meat and his swing is so open it doesn't have any power and he hits a real gentle, easy grounder out to first base and their first baseman fields it and Collins covers first and Chin's out.

Collins did it just right. Beautiful.

Our next two batters go down and we're into the bottom of the inning and they come to bat.

They go down, one two three, and here we are, seventh inning, scoreless tie, and I stop to size things up when I get to our bench, and I shake my head.

It's all backwards.

We're starting at the bottom of our batting order, - our four worst hitters, and, when they come to bat after us, we're facing the top of the batting order, - their best hitters.

And right then I know this thing is going to come down to the most important factor in baseball.

It's character.

When you've given it all you've got, and you feel like your well's dry, and you're standing there and you realize you got your worst hitters coming to the bat and they got their best, the only thing you got left is character. That's when you suck it all up and you set your jaw and you go to the well one more time. You don't know how you're going to get water when there isn't any left, but you don't quit and you don't back off -

you reach down clear past the bottom and you find what you got to have to win.

Webb's up first, then me, Denny, and Stone. Somehow we got to get through all four of us with only two outs, so we can start at the top of our lineup with our good hitters.

Webb hits a bouncer to shortstop and is thrown out at first.

I hit one to second base, and I'm thrown out, and I trot back to the bench.

I look at Denny. "You can do it. You can do it."

Denny licks his lips and picks out his bat and walks to the plate.

Second pitch, he connects and drives a blooper right over second base and pulls up safe at first.

We're still alive.

Stone picks out his little Easton and when he passes me I say quietly, "Come on, Stone, you can do it."

He takes his position in the batters box and looks out over his cocked left shoulder at Collins.

I look out there at Collins and I know exactly what's inside his head. He's pitched six tough innings, and he's wiping sweat and he's tired, and his arm is starting to go dead and his control is starting to go, and I know all this because I'm feeling the same things, and I know exactly what he's thinking when he looks at Stone.

Strike zone.

Stone's so little, he's got a strike zone about the size of a postage stamp, and Collins has got to be scared that he can't throw his good stuff with enough control to hit it. If Stone gets on base, either by a walk or a hit, Collins is looking at the top of our batting order where the good hitters are.

So it's decision time for Collins. Does he ease up a little so he can hit Stone's strike zone, or does he bear down and hope he has enough control to hit that little bitty strike zone with his best stuff?

He takes the sign and delivers, and the blue jerks his left hand and yells, "Ball".

Collins takes the throw from the catcher and turns and rubs the ball for a minute, then steps to the rubber and takes the sign and cranks up and delivers. I watch it all the way and it looks a whisper high to me and I hold my breath waiting for the blue.

"Ball tooh," calls the blue.

Their coach signals and they call time and the coach walks to the mound, and the infield comes in and they huddle for a minute. It looks like the coach is going to pull Collins, but he doesn't. While they're huddled, Stern calls Stone over.

"Wait him out. He'll walk you. Don't swing unless it's right where you want it."

Stone nods and walks back to the box to wait.

Their infield scatters to their positions and I watch, and they move back pretty good. Their third baseman's clear back on the grass, and so's their shortstop. Their second baseman's up close to his bag.

Collins steps to the mound and toes the rubber, and this time he doesn't take a sign from the catcher, and I suddenly know their coach has told him what to throw and how they figure to play it.

They know Stone's a pull hitter and usually hits to either shortstop or third base, and they know he can't hit too hard - I mean, what can you expect from eighty pounds - and we got Denny over on first base, and they know Denny runs okay, but he's not really fast.

So they figure to let Stone hit, and throw Denny out at second. That's why they got their shortstop and third baseman back - they don't want the ball to get behind them.

Collins ignores Denny's lead off and starts his wind up and I call to Stone, "EASY ONE RIGHT DOWN THE MIDDLE" and Collins can't stop his windup because if he does they'll call a balk and Stone will get a free walk to first. Collins delivers and it's an easy one right down the middle.

Stone hears me and he goes into his swing when Collins delivers and he meets the ball and we hear the "tink" and our whole bench stands as it arches out right towards the third baseman.

I'm holding my breath while it climbs and their third baseman takes a step backwards and leaps and the ball clears his mitt by one measured inch and drops thirty feet behind him and rolls to a stop in the grass.

Denny sprints at the sound of the bat and he rounds second just before the third baseman reaches the ball, and Denny isn't looking at Briggs coaching down on third, he's looking at their shortstop.

When the third baseman has to go for a grounder that gets behind him and there's someone coming from second into third, either the pitcher or the shortstop's got to hustle over and cover third. But their pitcher Collins hasn't moved a muscle, and their shortstop makes a mental error, and is standing there frozen, looking at the third baseman chase the ball.

Then Denny comes past him digging dirt at every stride, and suddenly the shortstop wakes up and starts for third, but he's playing catch up with Denny. Their third baseman gets the ball and pivots and sets to throw back to third and he has to check himself because nobody's at third!

The shortstop hollers "THROW THROW" and he's running as hard as he can and he's going to reach third just about when Denny does, and the third baseman underhands an easy toss, and the shortstop's looking to his right and he has to watch until he catches it, so he can't see Denny to his left, and he misjudges where Denny is and he starts to make his turn to tag Denny and instead he slams into him. He gets his mitt around and makes the tag on Denny but when he does his feet get tangled up with Denny's and he goes down in a heap and the ball flops out of his mitt and rolls into the grass behind third.

Denny stumbles a little but he doesn't go down, and he sees the ball skitter off in the grass, and he doesn't even break stride. He digs for home.

Their shortstop is quick and he leaps and pounces on the ball and cocks and throws for home and their catcher takes a giant step towards third to block Denny off the plate, and Denny is going full bore and he slides under the catcher's mitt and takes the catcher's legs out from under him and the ball smacks into the catcher's chest protector and bounces into the dirt just as Denny's toe reaches home plate. For just a second he lays there with their catcher laying flat on top of him, belly to belly, nose to nose through the catcher's mask.

"SAFE" bellows the blue.

While Denny's leaving all the wreckage behind at third base and headed for the collision at home, Stone buzzes right on around to third and hardly anybody noticed.

The catcher rolls off Denny and Denny gets to his feet and everyone in the bleachers is shouting, and me and Randy and Ned are yelling, "Awright, awright," and the rest of the team is making a little noise, but not much, but I don't care.

Denny dusts himself off as he comes around the chainlink and Ned whacks him on the back and I grin at him and we're saying, "Way to go, man, way to go," but Bernie and Chin and one or two others are standing a little ways off, not saying much. Mendoza's beside me, my old mitt on his hand while he tells Denny, "Great, man, great!"

Now we got a man on third, and Ned's our next batter, and we're over there praying. Just a single. Just get him home.

Ned pops out to second and we leave Stone stranded.

But there it is! Like I said, it's a crazy game, like life. You figure and you scheme, and you expect the heroes to do the job, but sometimes they don't and someone you'd never expect steps and does what's got to be done. Stone and Denny got us one lonely, freaky run, and we go into the bottom of the seventh with that skinny lead.

Now it's all on me.

I trot out to the mound and I rub the ball while our guys take their positions, and I look at their first batter. He's the top of their lineup and this kid hits about .380 and gets a lot of doubles.

I shake off Ned's curve ball sign and I take a fastball sign, and I crank up and deliver.

He swings and misses.

I do it again.

It don't matter that my arm's tired. They got to think I still got it all.

Ned signs and I deliver a looping curve and the batter swings and misses.

One down.

Their next batter steps up and Ned signs sinker and I deliver. The bottom falls out of the ball and the batter chases it down and gets the bat on it but there's no power in the hit and I field

79

it easy and throw to Chin.

Two down.

Their next batter comes up and I rub the ball a little while I get it all together. See, this kid's calm and he's a thinker, and he knows baseball, and I know that he and I are going to go to the mat before this is over.

I remember one thing about him.

He pulls a little when he hits hardest.

I take Ned's sign and deliver a looping curve and he lets it go and the blue calls, "Ball."

I deliver the second one, and it's three inches inside where the last one went and he pulls off it and this time the blue calls, "Steerike."

This kid looks at me and he doesn't grin, but he's unruffled and he's saying, that was good. Good.

I got to get ahead of this guy. I need a strike on the next one, real bad.

I shake off a curve sign and take a fastball sign, and I put one over belt high, but barely over the inside corner of the plate, right up against his hands. He hits belt high fastballs a mile and he can't resist this one, but it's too far inside and he comes around and pulls it just like I hoped, and I hold my breath as it arches out there in left field, and I watch it hook. It settles and I got my eye on the baseline, and it hits the ground two feet foul.

The blue calls, "Steerike".

I got the strike I had to have.

I suck air and exhale slowly while Stone relays the ball in from left field, and I think this over for a minute.

One ball, two strikes.

I shake off a sinker sign and take a fastball sign, and I deliver one a little high and on the outside edge. He's tempted, but he's disciplined and he let's it go.

"Ball," calls the blue.

I take Ned's curve sign, and I throw a high ball but I don't cock or twist my wrist much and it don't curve much, and Ned has to lunge up to even catch it.

Now we're three balls and two strikes, full count, and this kid looks at me steady, and takes his stance.

I call time.

Ned trots out. I say, "Curve."

Ned says, "That last one stank."

I say, "It stank on purpose. I got him set up. Curve."

Ned shrugs and trots back while I rub the ball.

I crank up and I throw one that starts out exactly like the last one, except this time I really twist my wrist over, and that sucker looks like it's going past Ned, clear to the backstop. This kid sees it and he starts to relax and step away.

When the ball's fifteen feet from the plate it starts to loop down to the left, and all of a sudden this kid realizes what's going on and he tries to snap back to his stance and swing, but he's too late, and he misses it a mile as it drops over the outside half of the plate.

"Steerike," yells the blue.

And it's over!

This kid's tight lipped, but he's under control and he glances at me and nods just a little, and he walks over to his bench while I walk over to mine. I beat him this time, but second half of the season, who knows?

There's a lot of noise in the stands, and there's some noise at our bench, with the exception of the white shorts bunch that ride limo's and Cadillacs to the park.

My head is slowly coming back from that other world where it goes when I'm locked in a duel like today and I got all my stuff going. I look around and here comes the Geezer with Mom beside him. I can't remember hearing one sound from either of them during the game but that could be because I didn't hear any sounds at all. That's all tuned out in a game like the one we just had.

The Geezer says, "That is what is called a baseball game."

I shrug. "Yeah." Why, oh why, couldn't he just once say, "Man, you did a job today. Really did a job." Sometimes I'd give anything to hear him say something like that. But all I get is a dumb statement that he could say to anybody.

Mom says, "Come help me with the cinnamon rolls," and she leads him off towards the parking lot. Mom doesn't have the foggiest idea that she has just seen a rare game.

I hear my name and turn, and it's Leo. He's been here to

watch the game because we play the Angels - his team - next, and I feel sorry for Leo because the Angels lost every game so far. He's a neat kid. Not too big, but an outstanding center fielder. An arm like a cannon, and a strong hitter. His team's just had a lot of bad breaks.

"Hi, Joe."

"Hi, Leo." I don't know what else to say for a minute. "See the game?"

"Yeah. Good game. You did great."

"Lucky."

"We play you guys pretty soon."

"Yeah. Two days."

"Well, see you around."

Coach calls, "All right, gather round."

The Geezer and Mom come back with six dozen of her home made cinnamon rolls, and Coach says, "Mrs. Russell has a treat for us."

Mom's cinnamon rolls are the kind they serve in heaven.

She stretches them and twists them before she puts them in the pan, and they look like they're braided. When they're baked, she pours sugar frosting over them while they're hot, and it kind of soaks in and puddles in the low places, and when you bite in, you get cinnamon and raisins and sugar frosting, and you sort of go brain dead for several seconds, and your eyes roll back in your head. In your sweetest dreams, you're eating Mom's cinnamon rolls.

"We'll talk while we eat," coach says.

Seventy two cinnamon rolls, ten guys, thats about six each when you take out some for the coaches. I watch while mom passes them out, and she gets down to Bernie and he shakes his head and glances away like he's saying, I don't eat common cinnamon rolls.

That ticks me off! I drop my mitt and I start over to get him straightened out when Mom does this funny thing.

She simply takes one off the big aluminum tray and puts it in his hand and keeps moving to the other guys.

I mean, what's he going to do? Toss it in the dirt? He's stuck. He has to do something with it. His face looks like he's got a bellyache while he painfully raises the cinnamon roll and takes a nibble.

And what happens next just knocks me cold!

He freezes for just an instant, and then he takes a bite, and then he jams the whole thing in his mouth and his eyes look like two pie plates and he trots over to Mom. His mouth's so full he can't talk, but he grabs two more and he smiles without opening his mouth and he looks sort of embarrassed, but that doesn't stop him.

He bolts that first one down, and for the first time I see Bernie grin, and I mean, when he grins, those teeth of his look like a piano keyboard!

I glance at Mendoza, and he looks like he's in hog heaven. He's got one in his mouth and one in each hand, and his eyes are closed and he's not hearing anything.

Coach talks. "We play the Angels day after tomorrow. We'll have a little skull drill tomorrow and light infield, maybe half an hour."

Mom stands there and beams. There's nothing in the world she likes more than baking something and then watching people tear into it like it's the best thing ever happened.

Coach finishes. "Be here at five. Thank Mrs. Russell."

The guys got frosting all over their faces and they're licking their fingers, but they all make a special trip to Mom to say thanks.

Chin walks up with his dictionary, and he thumbs to a page, and he reads, "Thank you, I was fortunate." Then he thinks, turns the page, and reads, "Thank you, I have had enough to eat."

He's got to work on that one.

I'm waiting to see how Bernie handles this, and again he knocks me out. He walks over to Mom and he says the magic words. "Can you bring some more?"

Mom just comes apart. "Of course."

"Thanks. Really. Thanks." And he gives Mom that keyboard grin, and I stand there like I been hit by lightning.

Stone comes over and thanks her, and when he walks away, I say, "Come on down to the field early tomorrow."

"What's up?"

"Work with Mendoza. Hitting."

"Mendoza?" He looks like he can't believe it. "Our Mendoza?"

"Yeah."

He looks real doubtful. "Okay."

We start gathering up the equipment. Mr. Stott's there, and I mean, this guy's a mountain! He walks, things tremble. But he's friendly and talking to the guys, and he helps us get the equipment into the bags.

Coach walks over to me. "Joe, you did good. A shut out."

"Denny won that one."

"He got our run, but you shut them out."

"Yeah. Lucky."

He smiles as we carry the equipment bag to his pickup.

At home, I shower and change, and I sit there on my bed thinking for a while, and then I go to the kitchen.

"Mom, could you bake cinnamon rolls a lot?"

"A lot?"

"Yeah. A few nearly every day?"

"What for?"

"Aw, just an idea," I say.

She raises her eyebrows and puts her hands on her hips. "How many?"

"I don't know. Maybe a dozen to start."

"For the team?"

"Yeah."

"Tomorrow?"

"Yeah."

CATASTROPHE

I'M STANDING THERE DRIPPING wet from the shower when Mom calls down the hall, "Phone."

A minute later I'm standing in the kitchen with a towel wrapped around.

"Hello."

"What's goin' on?"

It's Webb. "Nothing," I say.

"With Stone. What's goin' on?"

"Nothing much."

"He's coming to practice early?"

"Yeah."

"What's goin' on?"

"Just throw a few."

"Mendoza?"

"Yeah. He's coming too."

"What for?"

"Just throw a few."

"Oh. Okay," and he hangs up.

Ten minutes later I'm dressed and I pack my mitt and three old beat up baseballs wrapped in black tape in my backpack and tie my bat on my handlebars, and go back into the kitchen.

"You got those cinnamon rolls?"

Mom nods and hands me a brown paper bag with twelve wrapped in wax paper.

"Thanks."

Mendoza's waiting when I get to Griffith. I hand him the bat and get my mitt and the balls out of my back pack, and put the cinnamon rolls in, and give Mendoza a head sign, and he heads for home plate.

"Okay," I say. "Do what I say and I'll toss a few. Keep your eye on the ball, all the way. Keep your head down. Just try to hit the ball, not kill it. Just easy. Okay?"

He nods and I head out to the mound when Stone rides up on his bicycle. He walks over to the bench and looks at me.

I give him a head sign and say, "He's gonna hit a few. You shag."

He shrugs and walks out near third base, and we start.

I don't really pitch, I just lob them over easy while I watch him swing. Third swing, I'm amazed. He's the only human being I ever saw that did absolutely everything wrong. He hasn't touched a ball, and Stone's standing over there kicking his toe in the dirt with nothing to do.

I walk up to the plate and I say, "Okay, this time don't swing. Just watch the ball. Let it go past, but watch it all the way."

I go back to the mound, and Stone calls, "I'm going up behind the plate and catch."

I throw another one and Mendoza watches it go past and Stone throws it back. Three throws later I say to Mendoza, "Okay, this time, hit it real easy. Just bring the bat around and tap it."

He misses the next one, but the one after that he gets a piece of and the ball rolls out to me and he grins.

"Okay. Good."

Then he hits four out of eight, and I call to him, "Okay, harder."

He swings harder and misses, and I say, "You're closing your eyes. Keep your eyes open."

He swings and hits it and it rolls nearly to third base and I look at him and he's beaming. He finally got some kind of glimmer of understanding how you got to move your weight when you hit. You stride forward with your lead foot to get your weight going towards the ball and at the same time you swing, lead arm stiff and pulling, trailing arm stiff and pushing. The trick is to realize that when you stride, you lower the point of gravity of your body just a little, and you've got to swing just a little higher to compensate.

Mendoza? He's an expert on how not to bat. Getting him to put the bat on the ball is a world class achievement.

"What's goin' on?"

I turn at the voice behind me, and it's Webb. "Nothing."

"Oh. Okay."

He trots over to third and I continue to throw to Mendoza. Some he misses and Stone gets them, some he hits and Webb gets them. It's getting close to practice time and I say to Mendoza, "Okay, ten for score."

He grins and concentrates while I throw. He hits six of them. You'da thought he won the National League batting record. He's sweating and grinning, and I call to him, "Nice work. You're coming along."

We all walk to the big tree out behind third and turn on the hose for a drink while I watch the parking lot. Before we're through, the Cadillac pulls up and then the black limo, and I walk over to my backpack and get out the brown paper bag. I walk back to the shade and sit cross legged by the others and I open the bag, and I'm watching Chin and Bernie out of the corner of my eye.

I undo the wax paper and I take one of the cinnamon rolls and I look it over and I hand it to Mendoza, and then one for Stone and Webb. They're gone in ten seconds flat.

I divide the last eight, and I'm watching Chin and Webb, and I mean, they're standing there not moving a muscle while their eyes plead and their mouths water. But they don't say a thing and I don't either.

We pass around the hose again to wash our fingers and take another little drink, and I shove the wax paper and the old baseballs back in my pack as Stern's pickup rolls into the parking lot, and Briggs and the others are right behind him.

Coach calls us over. "Okay, listen up. It took a lot out of us to beat the Orioles, so we're going to be a little flat for the game tomorrow. Forget the Orioles. Think about the Angels. Get up for it. Okay. Briggs'll take the outfield."

We run infield and outfield drills for a while, and then coach calls us in for skull practice, and that's it.

"Tomorrow at four thirty," coach says, "and don't be late."

And that's it.

I get my mitt and bat and head for my bicycle when Bernie trots over, Chin right behind him.

"What was goin' on with Mendoza and Stone before?"

I shrug. "Nothing. Just tossing a few."

"Uuhhhh, any cinnamon rolls?"

I scrooch up my face like I'm thinking and I say, "Oh yeah. I forgot. Yeah."

Bernie nods and stands there, and Chin whips his book out of his hip pocket and runs his finger down a page and I wait while he silently mouths a couple words, and then he says, "The porridge looks very good."

Bernie looks disgusted and turns the page and fingers a line, and Chin looks and then reads, "May I have some more?"

I look puzzled. "More what?"

Chin looks at Bernie and then me, and then he says, without any help, "Cimmum rorrs."

I shrug. "Next time mom bakes."

Bernie's in pain. "When's that?"

"Few days."

Bernie nods and they walk away, and I peddle on home. When the Geezer gets home he gets out the batting tee.

"Your batting's down to about .270. Better get back to basics."

"Yeah. Right."

I take the bat, but when he's back in the house I take a half dozen disinterested swings and that's it. Why oh why couldn't he have just said, "Would it help to get the tee out? What do you think." He never does. He just says, do it do it do it.

Next day I finish at Earl's early and get home to clean up, and lay out flat and relax and think about the game.

The Angels have lost every game. The Blue Jays beat them nineteen to one. The game ended in the fifth inning on the ten rule. If a team's ahead ten runs at the end of the fifth, they win, and you don't play the last two innings. Leo's on the Angels, and I know he's so frustrated he gets red in the face talking about it. I talked with him, and we agreed we'd both give it the best we got, and after it's over, he's coming over to my place for a swim. The Angels got pretty good players, but so far they've made every error that can be made, and invented three that aren't in the books. Teams get in a slump and do that.

The Geezer comes home early and gets a sandwich, and we get in the car to go to Griffith, and while he's driving he says, "You didn't practice batting last night."

"Yeah, I did."

"What . . six swings?"

"More."

He looks mad and for a minute he's quiet.

"After the Orioles, your teams' going to be flat."

"Yeah. We'll be flat." Sometimes if I agree quick, he quits.

"Joe," he says, and there's a cutting edge in his voice, "you better sober up and get your head on straight. It doesn't matter if the Angels have been beat every game. You guys waltz in there with your heads scattered out, you'll get beat."

"Blue Jays beat them nineteen zip. We can beat them."

"Yeah, right." is all he says, and shakes his head in resignation.

He parks the car and goes to the bleachers while I trot out to the guys to start warming up. We pair up and start tossing balls to loosen up, and everybody's feeling good and there's talk.

Jackie's going to start, and if we get in trouble I can pitch the last three innings.

Coach calls us over. "Listen up. You're going to be a little flat. Concentrate. Forget the Orioles. These guys would eat glass to beat us, so get your heads together. You lose, it's because you didn't get serious. Humble up. Let's see some snap, some hustle."

We go out and show some snap and hustle but there's no sense getting really psyched for this one.

"Batter up," shouts the blue,

They're home team so we bat first.

We go down, one two three.

Their first guy comes up and Jackie throws the first pitch and the guy creams it - a home run.

Their next guy bangs out a double, their next guy another one, and their next guy, a triple.

They got three runs and a guy on third and no one's out!

Jackie's standing on the mound like he's shellshocked.

Their next guy hammers another home run out past Bernie in left, and they got five runs in the first inning and still no outs.

Coach signals time and we trot to the bench.

"Better get serious," is all he says and we nod.

They send eleven batters to the plate in that first inning, and eight of them score.

I mean, nothing is in sinc for us. Jackie's missing the plate a foot, Ned's dropping the ball, the infield's booting easy grounders, us guys in the field can't catch, and by the end of the inning we're so shook we can hardly find the bench.

Two innings later the score is eleven zip.

Jackie throws a perfect strike and Ned misses it and it goes clear to the screen, and Ned whips off his mask and pivots to sprint after it and plows into the blue, and they go down, and while Ned scrambles to get the ball another run scores.

Randy drops to one knee to pick up an easy grounder and he blows it, and he tries again and gets it and starts to throw, and he fumbles it again, and this time he just kicks it over to second, at Webb.

Their pitcher is a nice, gentle kid named Rich and he delivers one to Ned like it's on a silver platter and Jimmy swings Olympic class and doesn't come close. Next two pitches, same thing, and Ned strikes out, and he puffs up like a big bull snake and I'm afraid he's going to throw his helmet and get ejected. He catches his temper just in time.

Randy goes down swinging.

Chin swings three times and he's out.

Bottom of the fourth, the score is twelve to zero. We're going to lose this thing on the ten run rule if we don't get over this crappy streak.

Top of the fifth, for the first time their pitcher looks tired and pitches like he's laboring and he walks the first two of our guys. Ned finally hits a single and the two guys on base score and we got two runs, nobody out, Ned on first base. The pitcher throws a wild pitch and Ned makes third before their catcher can find it.

We all start to breathe again, because we won't lose on the ten run rule if we can get Ned home, and I can shut them down the second half of the fifth.

Randy comes up.

He runs it to a full count, three and two and then he manages to get a good, solid liner right down third base line deep into left field, a sure triple, and Randy really turns on the gas. Ned crosses the plate from third as Randy rounds first and heads for second and he sees the left fielder still chasing the ball and pounds on down to third and he sees the fielder making his throw and he figures he can stretch the triple to a home run. He doesn't look at the coach as he rounds third, and he rips for home.

Their cut off man takes the throw and pivots and relays, and Randy slides as the ball whips over his head and the catcher takes it and drops to block Randy, and he puts the mitt on him and the blue is right there.

His hand jerks up. "Yer OUT".

Randy can't believe it. He jumps up and starts towards the blue and then catches himself and turns towards the dugout. He whips off his helmet and throws it against the chain link. The blue looks at him and shakes his head and jabs his thumb in the air.

"You're outta here."

Randy? Our quiet, gentle, friendly shortstop, has been ejected for temper? Impossible! There is no argument, no appeal. Randy's gone and I'm holding my breath to see what coach does, because when Randy rounded third, Coach had both palms against him to hold third, do not try for home, but Randy didn't even look.

Coach doesn't say a word. Randy passes him and coach whacks him on the back side like always, and Randy drops to the bench and locks his head in his hands and sits there.

Their pitcher hits Chin with a pitched ball and Chin takes

first, and Bernie raps one to the short stop, who doubles Chin on second and Bernie on first.

Top of the fifth is over. Score is now twelve to three.

If I can stop them these last three innings, and if their pitcher is tired enough, maybe we got a shot at getting the ten runs we need to win this thing.

With Randy gone, coach puts me on the mound, Jackie goes to shortstop, Bernie comes from right field to center field, and then coach has no choice. He sends Mendoza out to right field, and I see Mendoza's face beaming as he trots past me.

Their first batter steps up and I take the sign from Ned.

Fastball, right over the plate, six inches high, ball one.

I know right then that I'm out of sinc.

Ned signs another fast ball and it smacks into his glove four inches outside, ball two.

I take the third sign. Curve.

My high looper drops in and hits the batter on the forearm, and he's on first base free!

I feel sweat on my upper lip and my stomach's a knot, and I rub the ball and walk around the mound, and I look at the other guys and their faces are white and drawn, and we're all rattled so bad we couldn't catch a ball in a bushel basket.

Next batter steps up.

Six pitches later, the blue calls, "Ball four", and this guy walks to first and now they got two runners, and no outs.

Nothing's working right! My brain and my arm are in two different galaxies.

Their next batter is Leo, and he steps up, dead pan, and cocks the bat and he's ready.

Ned calls for a sinker and I deliver but it starts to sink way too late and Leo comes around and connects solid and the ball's a blur headed out between Denny and Bernie in the outfield. It hits and rolls and Bernie runs it down and scoops it up as the first runner crosses the plate.

Bernie turns to make his throw, and all of a sudden the ball squirts out of his mitt, three feet over his head and he loses sight of it and can't figure where it went until it comes down. The second runner crosses the plate as he scoops it up and throws hard to Randy at the cutoff, but the throw is low and

Randy has to short hop it and he bobbles it, and barehands it out of the dirt and turns while Leo's sprinting for home. Randy loads and fires, and the ball sails five feet over Ned's head and hits the backstop.

Leo cross the plate standing.

Score? Fourteen to three.

"Games over," hollers the blue. "Ten run rule. Angels win."

I stand there numb. I lost the game! I gave the Angels, the doormats of the league, two unearned runs and a home run on errors - I gave them the game!

I stand there for a minute unable to figure out what to do and then I start for the bench and the other guys come dragging in. Coach shoves us into a line to give their team a high five while we walk past each other, and I can hardly look at them.

In shocked silence we start gathering up the equipment and stuffing it into the big bags, and coach comes over and starts tossing helmets in with me. He doesn't say anything until the helmets are in the bag and I start to draw the big strings to close it.

"You start next game, Joe."

I wish he'd shout and storm and everybody would hear it, but he doesn't. He turns and walks away, and it's over.

Leo catches me while I'm walking to the car with the Geezer.

"Joe, about coming over tonight for a swim, . . " I see he's trying to make it easy on me.

"Hey, you're coming on over," I say. "You played great. Big league hit in the seventh."

He looks serious for a minute. "Okay. Just after supper."

"We're going to have hamburgers off the grill. Come on over and eat with us. We got extra."

"I'll be over in half an hour."

The Geezer smiles at him and we continue walking while he trots over to his bicycle.

On the ride home the Geezer hums a little ditty like he does and drums his fingers on the steering wheel. When we get close to home he says, "Batting average is down a little right now. About .248."

Batting! I gave away a game, busted our perfect season record, and he's talking batting average! There's no way I'm going to talk to him. I just sit there with my teeth gritted.

He parks the car and pulls the keys out. "Got to get back to basics."

If I hear it once more I'll throw up.

I open the door and start for the house.

THE COMEBACK

I GET HOME FROM EARL'S roof about three and by three thirty I'm laying on my bed cooling off from a hot shower when Mom calls down the hall, "Phone."

"Hello."

"You guys gonna meet before practice?"

It's Bernie!

"Yeah."

"Okay."

He hangs up and I turn to Mom. "Better pack about a dozen cinnamon rolls. Make it fifteen."

At four o'clock I'm at Griffith and Mendoza's waiting, and Stone and Webb show up on their bikes, and while we're walking out to the field, this fancy motor scooter pulls up and Bernie takes off his crash helmet. Two minutes later the black aircraft carrier stops and Chin trots over to the ballfield. I don't say anything and neither do they.

Mendoza goes to the plate with my bat and Stone squats behind the plate, and Webb takes shortstop, and Bernie and Chin take up positions on second and first.

Mendoza's scared. I mean, here we got half the team there to teach him, and in his whole life, nobody has ever taken time to teach him anything because he's fat and slow, and maybe a little because he's Hispanic.

"Okay," I say, "forget us. Forget everything but the ball. Keep your eye on it."

I lob easy and he starts hitting more and more of them, and the guys field them. He sweats like always, and after while I say, "Stone, why don't you take the bat, and Webb, you catch, and Mendoza, take third."

Mendoza swallows and points at his own chest, and I say, "Yeah. You."

He gets the old mitt I gave him and takes third and I can see he's terrified, with all those other guys around him.

Webb lays one down to him and he bumbles it and nobody says anything. Webb taps one out to Chin and he fields it. Then Webb knocks an easy one to Mendoza and Mendoza puts down the knee and this time he nails it and comes up and transfers and throws to me, and it's a little wide but I catch it and I don't say nothing, but he's beaming.

We keep it up. Pretty soon Mendoza's getting most of them, and the sweat's running and I say, "Nearly five o'clock. We better knock it off."

"Naw," Mendoza calls, "let's practice."

I throw a couple more and Mendoza fields them, and I glance at Bernie, and he's getting nervous about the other guys coming, and the cinnamon rolls in my backpack.

"Let's knock off," I say, and head for the hose and the shade. We all sit cross legged, and the six of us divide up fifteen cinnamon rolls and drink hose water and wait for the team. I notice that this time Bernie eats slow, and he's on another planet with his eyes closed. Chin doesn't talk while he eats his "cimmum rorrs".

The rest of the guys arrive and coach calls us to the bench.

"Mental," he says. "We let down mentally because the Angels were supposed to be easy. We're four and one right now, tied with the Orioles. We play the Cubs tomorrow and the Orioles play the Angels in the game after ours. We can still be champs of the first half season if we win and the Orioles lose, so let's get at it."

We all start picking up our mitts and he stops us for one

more minute.

"Anger can be useful."

He's talking about Randy losing his temper and getting eject-ed yesterday.

"Control it. Put it to work."

We go at it serious, focused, concentrated, with little talk.

After practice I peddle home and the Geezer's there, out in the garage. He comes in and washes his hands and then comes out in the kitchen where I'm drinking orange juice.

"How was practice."

"Okay."

"You guys got your heads together?"

"Yeah."

"You going to use the tee tonight?"

"Yeah."

I get braced for his lecture, but it doesn't come. He just sits down at the dinner table and opens the newspaper. After sup-per I set up the batting tee and I hit one hundred balls. Then I take the old taped ones and I pick out a cinderblock in the back wall, and I throw thirty times and I hit it twenty eight.

Heavy clouds move in that night and next morning we got a soft summer rain. Earl calls to say we can't work on the roof in the rain, and I got the day to myself, until game time. I sit down at the dinner table with a pad and pencil and I jot down the things I remember about each of their hitters. How they stand, what they can hit, what they can't hit, do they pull, -everything I can recall.

About one o'clock the rain stops and around three the clouds break and sunshine comes through. I'm getting pretty nervous with nothing to do so I peddle down to Griffith to see if the infield's too wet to play, and it's sticky but there are no puddles. It'll probably be okay by game time. I peddle back home and lay down for a while, and then get ready, and the Geezer comes home and mom gets ready, and we drive on down to Griffith.

The guys are all there before four thirty so we take the field for warmups, and then they take it and I watch their warmup. Their coach is the big guy that did the tryouts, Will Shellins, and he's a tough coach and he's trained a tough team.

We're home team so they bat first.

The blue hollers "Batter up," and we go out to the field. The ground's a little damp but it's firm. No problem.

I know after the first pitch that I'm not in top form, but it's okay. I'm concentrating and I keep saying to myself, one pitch, one batter at a time. One at a time.

At the end of the fourth inning we're ahead, three to one. It's in the fifth that this game comes to pieces.

Their first guy up is a strong hitter, but he's also big, and a bully and he shoots off his mouth a lot, and I'm sick of him. I call time and huddle with the coach, and we agree. The next two batters after this guy are weak, and I think I can set up a double play if we put him on first, and the coach says okay. Walk him.

Ned signs the pitchout and I toss three easy balls when I hear the voice from the bleachers.

"Joe, throw strikes."

It's mom. The Geezer talks to her while everyone else chuckles and I play like I didn't hear.

One pitch later he's on first base and he's got that ugly mouth of his going. He's giving Chin fits, and he's calling really rotten things to me, and I ignore him.

The next batter comes up, and I move him back with a fast-ball inside and then make him reach for a curve over the out-side edge of the plate and he taps it right back to me, just like I figured. I field it and turn and make my throw to Webb on second, easy play, and that's when things get hot. Here comes this big guy like a freight train, and he slides.

Sliding is an art, not just an act. You can do it like Pete Rose did it - head first - and if you do you take whatever's in front of you smack in the face. Or you can slide feet first, and when you do that, you go down on one side and you hook for the bag with your down foot, and you try to interfere with the guy on the base with the other one. The problem is, you can't inter-fere too much or the ump calls you out, so you learn you can get that up side leg just so high and no higher.

Well, this big bozo comes sliding feet first and his up leg's about four feet high and aimed straight at Webb and when Webb takes my throw he starts to touch second base and make his throw to Chin, but this guys foot catches Webb's arm! It knocks the ball loose and tips Webb staggering sideways.

Man, I mean, I throw my mitt down and I wait for the base ump to call this guy out, and all our guys are shouting "eject eject eject" but the base ump shakes his head.

I can't believe it!

Coach Stern calls time and gathers us around. "Bad call. Choke it down and stay cool. Best way to get revenge is beat these guys. Do it."

We all go back to our positions and I size up this next batter and he's one of their worst.

I move him back with an inside fastball and then I throw him another one that's just barely over the plate, right by his hands, and he tries to swing but it's too close to get anything on it and he knocks a dribbler out to Randy, just like I figured it.

Easy double play. Randy will throw to Stone on third, and Stone will throw to Webb and we got a double play, and we're out of trouble.

But here comes that big hero and he's bearing down on Stone, and we stand frozen while he goes into that slide again. His up foot is about four feet high, and this time it catches Stone square in the chest and it knocks him five feet behind the base! The ball goes rolling and Stone's on the ground, grabbing his chest and we can hear him trying to get his breath.

I throw down my mitt and start for third and I hear noises behind me and I turn my head to look, and it just knocks me cold.

It's Bernie!

I mean, here's this rich guy that's so snobby he hasn't said hardly anything to anybody the whole season, and he's breathing smoke and fire and running hard. He gets about ten feet from this big guy and he throws his mitt right in the guy's face and I slant right and grab Bernie just before he gets to the guy and I try to hold him, and Randy comes past me like a cannonball and plows straight into the guy and Webb's right on top of both of them windmilling at this guy.

Their bench empties and here come their players like a herd of buffalo and I hear a high Kung Fu yell and Chin takes out two of their guys and Jackie grabs another one and tears half his shirt off, and Denny grabs another guy and wrestles him to the ground, and here comes Mendoza from the bench, and he falls on one of their guys and the guy's done for the day, and I let go of Bernie and he grabs a guy and I grab a guy and I mean, we got one of the best baseball brawls I ever saw.

Right in the middle of it I hear this foghorn from the bleachers.

"JOE, YOU BE CAREFUL."

It's Mom!

The blues come charging in, and both coaches, and then the Geezer and the Mountain come running, and they start shoving us towards our benches, and finally they get us all sorted out. The blues gather up all the mitts and baseball caps, and three shoes, and the plate ump marches back to home plate and quiets everybody down.

"The baserunner at third is out and he's ejected from this game. He does that again, he's finished for the season."

He looks at Stone. "You okay? Can you play?"

Stone nods and his voice is high and whispery. "Yeah. You bet. Sure. Let's go."

The ump looks at both coaches and they nod and he bellows, "Play ball."

I take out their next two batters on called strikes, and in the sixth and seventh we take them in order, and we score one more run and we win it, four to one.

The worst we can do is tie for champs of the first half of the season. If the Angels beat the Oriole's, we win the championship outright.

Our parents in the bleachers raise a roar, and the team jumps around and yells, and Coach Stern settles us down and makes us walk through the line for trading high fives with the Cubs, and things get a little quiet, but when we're through someone grabs the hose over by the trees and starts squirting all of us and Ned tries to get the hose and pretty soon there's a wrestling match and we're all wet and yelling.

Man, I mean we're a mess, and we don't care.

None of us goes home. We wait for the game between the Angels and the Orioles, and we stay through the whole thing. The Angels win it, five to four, and man alive, I mean, we pound them on the back, and Webb turns on the hose again, and before it's finished we're all covered with mud and we're dripping water.

I find Leo. "Nice game. Neat."

He grins. "That's the way it goes."

The Geezer finally tells me to gather up my stuff, and we go home. I finish in the shower and come back out, and my arm's tired, and I hurt where I tackled that guy, but it's all kind of a mellow feeling. Mom sets out a chicken sandwich and milk, and I drop into the chair while she's on the phone, and start on the sandwich.

Then I hear what she's saying.

"Mrs. Billman? This is Mrs. Russell. Yes, Joe's mother. Oh thank you, please call me Margaret. Claire, we're going to have a party for the team at our place, next Friday night. Yes. Yes. Oh would you? Bring your family. It's a family affair. Six oclock sharp. We'll do barbeques."

She hangs up and I'm choking on chicken. "What're you doing?"

"Coach said we should have a get together of the team and their families to celebrate winning the first half of the season."

"Bernie? And Chin?"

"Of course."

"And Mendoza?"

"Certainly."

"Everybody and their families together here at one time?"

"Absolutely."

I see the Chin aircraft carrier and the Billman Mercedes pulling up in front of the house with the Mendoza flatbed rattletrap truck in between, with about twenty kids hanging out, and my brain goes into gridlock.

10

A PARTY TO REMEMBER

"WHY CLAIRE, HOW NICE TO see you. Here. Let me take that."

I'm out near the pool, getting ready to slap hamburger patties on the hot grill, and I got this dumb apron on that Mom makes me wear, and I lean back to see what the Billman family looks like.

Claire Billman is a classy looking lady, and she comes off cool and confident and in charge. Dr. Billman is tall and wears a starched, long sleeved white shirt and paisley tie, and looks like he stepped out of a show window and like he's sitting in judgment on everything he sees. He's carrying the big platter.

"He'll take it to the kitchen," Claire says, and I get the feeling she isn't going to let anyone but Dr. Billman touch this enormous, heavy, cut crystal platter of fresh fruits, covered with saran wrap. I wonder who she hired to do all the peeling and cutting.

Mom leads them to the kitchen and she points and Dr. Billman sets it down and they walk back through the archway to the front room.

I see past them out the open front door and the aircraft carrier pulls up and Chin and an older girl get out, and then this little lady that looks like a China doll, and a man that's blocky and looks just like Chin, and the little man gets a big silver platter of something from the back seat and they walk to the house.

Mom hurries to the front door and says, "Ming, so glad you could come! Let me take the serving tray."

Ming looks at Chin and he runs a finger down a page of his book and says something in Chinese and his Mom shakes her head no and points, and mom leads her and Mr. Chin to the kitchen. He puts down the platter and it's filled with every kind of Chinese cookie and cracker ever invented.

Ming bows and shakes Mom's hand and looks pleased and bewildered, and she keeps bowing and she doesn't understand very much, so Mom keeps talking and pretty soon Ming looks a little relieved and they all walk back into the front room with the others. Mr. Chin shakes hands and his face is like stone, but his eyes catch everything. Chin translates for them with his pidgin English book and pretty soon things sort of mellow out and people stop being so stiff and a little chatter begins.

The guys shove their hands in their pockets and amble through the kitchen searching, and come on out to the area around the pool. I'm at the grill in one corner, and there are tables and chairs around the other end of the pool where the diving board is, and a big buffet table with everything you can put on hamburgers.

Stone gets here and brings his sister and brother, and his Mom has a big plate of fancy cut melons, and the Stotts arrive with their five kids and a plate of dips, and I'm wondering about Ned and Jackie, and then I hear it.

Two blocks away, the sound of a V-6 Chevy truck engine with one cylinder clattering and the muffler nearly disconnected. The faded, battered old one ton flatbed pulls up in front and the engine shuts off and it keeps firing for about ten seconds and then backfires and wheezes and dies.

Mr. Mendoza gets out and goes around and helps out this plumpy woman, and she's got a baby in her arm and a toddler by the hand, and Mendoza jumps off the flatbed and helps ten more kids down, one at a time. Dad starts for the house and Mama lines up behind him and they all string out behind Mama in order of age except Mendoza. He's carrying a big clay bowl of something, and he brings up the rear to catch stragglers.

Fifteen Mendozas. Each of the kids is dressed in dark pants or a dark skirt and a white shirt or blouse, and the boys have a kitchen bowl haircut and the girls have one long braid down their backs, and their shoes are all hand me downs and someone's used about three cans of shoe polish trying to put some life into them.

Mom meets them at the door, and I hold my breath to see how this works out.

"Rosa, how nice you could bring your family." Mom clasps her hands and takes the big clay bowl from Mendoza and hands it to the Geezer, and she shakes the hand of the Mother, and the Mother introduces everybody in the family. The husband is Juan, and the ten year old daughter is Maria, and Mendoza's first name is Felipe, but from there I don't get a single name. Pedro, Pablo, Paula, - they all run together.

I'm watching to see what happens when the Mendozas start to mix with the Billmans and the Chins. They walk to one side of the room and the kids line up behind Mom and Dad and they stand there with downcast eyes like they're afraid to look at anybody. Then the baby goes red faced and I hear this little sound, and then there's this grunty sound, and a muffled sound, and the baby smiles and looks relieved.

Mom's right on top of it. "Let me help you," she says to Rosa, and leads her up the hall to the nearest bathroom and Maria follows with the diaper bag. Mrs. Billman examines a painting Mom's got above the piano, and Ming says something quietly to Chin, and then the coaches arrive with their wives, and Jackie and Ned. The Geezer carries all the food from the kitchen out to the buffet by the pool, and the rest of the Mendoza army follows him out and their eyes get big and they stand there still and quiet and I can tell they never seen that much food at one time in their lives, and they can't believe the swimming pool.

Mendoza walks over and says, "Hi."

"Hi."

"Can I help?"

"Naw. One man job."

I pause to look at him. "What does your Dad do?"

"Runs the crane in the pit."

"Oh. Yeah. Big machine."

"Yeah. Dad works it good. He's teaching me."

I glance at him and I can see the pride.

And I look at Bernie, and I'm standing there thinking, Bernie's got everything money can buy, anything he'll ever want, but I've never seen that look in his eyes about his family. So who's got it best at home? Mendoza or Bernie? I work on that for a minute, but the answer isn't easy, and there's no time to sit down and study on it, so I store it for later.

Coach arrives and I cover the grill with hamburger patties that smoke and sputter, and the guys all stand around swallowing and looking over at the sliced tomatoes and onions and mustard and ketchup and relish, and then back at the patties.

By now there's polite conversation starting between the grownups, and the guys have all gone into the kitchen for a drink of water while they search out the cinnamon rolls that are still on great big cookie sheets in the oven, and the Coach and the Geezer talk for a while, and I get about fifty hamburger patties done and stacked to one side in the warmer with four dozen buns.

Coach says, "Ready?" and Mom says "Yes."

Coach walks to the diving board end of the pool where everything's set up and stands at the head table and calls everybody to take a place, and the families gather at the tables. The guys come sit on a bunch of folding chairs down one side of the pool near me and the hamburgers.

"Thank you all for coming. Before we eat, there are a few very important things we should talk about. I promise it won't take long."

There's the magic words! No adult ever gave a big old long speech without first promising it wouldn't be a big old long speech.

"We've come a long ways and we're doing fine. There are just a few things we should be working on to improve."

Five minutes later I heave a big sigh and I look at Webb and Randy and they roll their eyes with boredom and they're getting restless.

Coach drones on. "Our worst problem is believing in

our selves."

Randy looks at me and I read something in those dark eyes and he whispers. "I bet Bernie can eat more hamburgers than anyone else on the team."

I think for a minute. "You're on."

"Who?," he asks.

"Mendoza."

His eyebrows arch. "Yeah. That oughta be good."

"When do we go," I asked.

"Right now," he says, and I grin.

"What does the winner get," I ask.

"Nothin'. Loser gets wet."

"Tell Bernie and Mendoza."

He whispers to Stone and Stone whispers to Webb and Webb whispers to Mendoza and Bernie, and they both nod. They're sitting behind Jackie and Ned and Denny and Randy and can't be seen too easy by the guys up by the buffet.

I'm sitting right by the warmer on the grill and I quietly slip a patty into two buns and the guys pass them behind their backs, and Bernie and Mendoza start, and the race is on.

"We started this season with little hope . . ." Coach keeps fogging the air with his really short talk. Everybody else is looking at him or at the big pile of eats on the buffet table and not paying attention to us guys. By now six hamburgers have gone out, three each.

Coach continues. "We only have three more games. We are peaking just about right."

The guys are glancing sideways at Bernie and Mendoza who are cramming hamburgers in as fast as they can. The Geezer sees the sideways glances and he senses something's wrong and he looks at me with a frown. I give him my best smile like, nice day, and he turns back to coach, but he knows something's up.

Two more hamburgers go out and Bernie and Mendoza are in a dead heat.

"If we win the second half like we did the first, we don't even have to face a playoff."

Bernie is chewing furiously while Mendoza just bites and swallows.

Two more hamburgers go out.

"Man for man, position for position, player for player, we have a pretty good team. We have good team leaders."

I send out two more hamburgers and watch Bernie. He's showing the first signs of slowing, but Mendoza is still biting and swallowing like a machine.

By now the guys are all glancing sideways and Jackie and Jimmy and the ones in the front row are twisting their heads to look every few seconds, and pretty soon some of the parents look like they're suspicious but no one can see what's going on and no one does anything.

"So I have just a few suggestions to move us towards the championship."

Two more hamburgers. Randy holds up all ten fingers and then four. Fourteen so far, seven each.

"First, think about the game that's coming. Forget all the games you've won, or lost, in the past. Just think about the one that's before you."

Two more hamburgers. Randy shows all ten fingers and six more. I look and there's a big hole in the hamburger stack in the warmer.

I send two more hamburgers.

"And my last suggestion is, we support each other. No one on the team criticizes any one else on the team for their mistakes. A positive statement beats any negative statement."

By now no one on the team is listening to coach. They can't believe these two guys have put down sixteen hamburgers, and they're all turning to see if either one of them can choke down this last one.

Mendoza bites and jams number nine in just as Bernie starts on his.

Coach says, "Thank you for your attention," and sits down.

Polite applause starts while people start getting up and Randy signals and Webb grabs Mendoza and Bernie by the shoulder and says, "Stop," and they both stop chewing and the team stands and we huddle around Bernie and Mendoza.

Neither one has a hamburger in their hand, but they both have what's left of the last one in their mouth and they quit chewing when Webb grabbed them.

I look at Randy. "I guess the one with the most left in his

mouth loses."

Randy thinks for a minute. "Yeah."

He grabs Bernie and we look in his mouth, and then we grab Mendoza and look in his.

I look at Randy and he looks at me.

"Tie?" I ask him.

"Dead heat", he says.

I look around to see if any parent has figured it out and they haven't a clue. They're up there congratulating coach, and getting ready to eat.

"Who gets wet?," says Randy.

I think a minute. "Neither one, or both. Which?"

A grin slides across Randy's face and he looks at the rest of the guys and they start grinning, and suddenly Bernie's eyes get big and Mendoza starts to say something, and we all grab both of them.

Bernie hits the water first and Mendoza second. Bernie floats pretty good, but Mendoza goes down like a submarine. Bernie starts for the edge, and the whole team's standing around in hysterics, and the parents gasp and they don't know what happened. Then all of a sudden Rosa yells something in Spanish and runs to the edge of the pool and points down, and no one understands.

Maria runs to her and says something in Spanish, and Rosa says something hysterical, and Maria turns to us and shouts, "HE CAN'T SWIM."

I hit the water first and about four other guys are right behind me and we go down, and there's Mendoza, standing on the bottom, and I swear, he's chewing that last hamburger.

Ever try to beach a whale?

We finally roll him up on the edge of the pool, and he's laying there with water running everywhere, and his mother's wailing, "He's dead he's dead."

The Geezer gets him onto a chair, and Dr. Billman walks over and looks confused and doesn't do anything because he's a brain doctor and doesn't know about drownings, so Mendoza's Dad grabs his arms and starts pumping, and all of a sudden Mendoza starts to chew the rest of the hamburger in his mouth, and his mother grabs a cheek in each hand and shouts mouth, and his mother grabs a cheek in each hand and shouts something in Spanish.

He swallows the last of the hamburger and nods. "Si."

The guys go hysterical.

Then the Geezer and the Mountain and Dr. Billman, and the Coach and half the parents gather round us, and we look at them, and they look really dark, and things die down while we await the execution.

Coach says, "Accident? They fell in?"

I look at Randy and then back at coach. "Uh, no. We threw them in."

"Why?"

"A bet."

"Okay, let's have it."

So I start to tell him and then Randy chimes in, and then Bernie gets into it and then he rest of the guys, and by that time the parents start to grin and then to laugh, and before it's over they're in stitches. Even Claire Billman cracks a smile, and Dr. Billman turns away to hide his grin.

I take a deep breath. That was close.

Mom gets towels and I slap a whole new batch of hamburgers on the grill.

Ten minutes later we're pulling off hot hamburgers and everybody's still laughing, and the pile of food is steadily going down.

I walk over to see what Rosa brought in that clay Mexican bowl, and it's guacamole. I get a big tortilla chip and dip it, and I mean, that's the best guacamole in the history of the world!

The women go into the kitchen and politely swap recipes for guacamole and cinnamon rolls and Chinese cookies, and it's starting to get dark. I keep frying hamburgers.

Pretty soon Maria whispers something to Mendoza, and he shakes his head no.

"What's she want," I ask.

He looks embarrassed. "Nothing."

"Bathroom's right down the hall."

"No. No bathroom."

I stop and look at him. "What then?"

"To swim."

I think that one over and I call Mom. She listens, and then she walks over to Rosa and they talk for a minute and Rosa shakes her head violently and mom talks some more and finally Rosa nods.

Mom steps up by the diving board.

"The little children would like to swim but they didn't bring suits. I said it's okay if they go in their underwear. I do hope no one will be offended. I have a basket of swimming suits for any of the other youngsters who want to go in."

Mom disappears and comes right back with a big wicker basket with about thirty old swim suits that were left by the people the Geezer bought the house from, and the team and all their brothers and sisters sort through them and the girls go to one bedroom and the guys to another, and ten minutes later we're all in the water. The two smallest Mendoza kids don't have suits, so they just go in without anything on. Mendoza takes the baby in his arms and lets him splash around and I don't remember ever seeing pleasure like in the eyes of the Mendoza army in that pool. Darkness settles in and we turn on the pool lights, and it's a long time before we all climb out and use a pile of towels getting dried off.

Mom divides the few left over cinnamon rolls equal and wraps them in Reynolds and gives them to the guys, and then she gets out big paper plates and portions out the leftovers to all the parents, and we all move out to the street. The Geezer turns on the front yard flood lights and we stop and gab and slowly they drift on out to their cars, carrying the leftover food plates, and Mom stands out there and waves each one off, and they all wave back.

The Mendoza's are the last to leave.

Rosa counts her brood and Maria carries the baby asleep on her shoulder and Mendoza carries the food, and Rosa starts to say goodbye to Mom, and she suddenly starts to cry and Mom hugs her and she hugs Mom back, and then Rosa follows her husband to the beat up truck and Mendoza hoists the kids up onto the flatbed. The old Chevy sputters and starts, and they chug for home with one headlight missing.

I go back to clean up the grill, and the Geezer comes out to put away all the chairs and clean up the buffet table with mom, and when we finish, he pauses.

"That was pretty bad judgment, throwing those two in the

water."

Here it comes.

"Yeah."

"You could have hurt Mendoza."

"We didn't."

"Well, it was bad judgment."

It was a great party and it's all over and everybody's okay and everybody else thought it was funny, so why have I got to stand here and take this garbage from the Geezer? For once, why couldn't he just grin and say, "Kinda dumb, what you idiots did, but it was kinda funny, too." Why couldn't he do it, just once?

I shrug and I don't say anything because I don't know anything to say. I just hate standing there getting beat up on.

11

WE'RE DEAD. SEE, SECOND half of a baseball season, everything changes.

First off, everybody's played everybody once, so everybody knows we caught the league by surprise the first half, but the surprise is over. They'll be ready for us the second half, and we're dead.

Second, we don't play the teams in the same order as the first half, which means we might get the easy teams first and the tough ones last, or vice versa.

Third, and maybe most important, teams change, you know, peak out. If you use up all your juice during the season and you're burned out for the playoffs, all you got is a great record and no gas for the stretch. We won't peak out because the team's divided. We got rich and poor, good players and bad, and they never do stuff together, you know, hang around, go to the movies once in a while, stuff where you get to know how the other guys think.

The morning after the big party at our house I go on down to Earl's roof and we cook and pour tar and spread gravel until three, and I'm sweated out. I pedal home and shower and change and die on my bed for half an hour before I eat the sandwich and milk Mom sets out, and at four o'clock I pedal to the field for practice.

"Okay, listen up," coach says, "we're going to do some new things. Ned, you're going to pitch a few, and Bernie, you're going to catch him."

Coach stops and looks around. "Where's Bernie?"

We all look, and he's not there.

"Okay," says coach, "Joe, you warm Ned up." He stops for a minute before he lays it on us. "And I want Mendoza to get ready for backup in right field."

Mendoza freezes and his eyes got that one thousand yard stare like he's been hit in the forehead by a fastball. I look at him and shrug my shoulders, like, big deal, you can handle it easy, and he swallows hard.

I take Ned over by the big tree behind our bench and ask, "Ever pitch before?"

"Just goofin' around."

"Know how to grip the stitches for each kind of pitch?"

He shrugs. "Sort of."

I show him and make him do it a couple times and then I back off a ways.

"Throw easy thirty times," I tell him, "don't start trying a fastball for a day or two."

He throws easy and he's got a good motion except his kick isn't high enough because he's been a catcher and they don't use a kick at all, they throw all arm. So I talk with him a minute and then he gets it better, and pretty soon he's starting to look like he might be okay.

I glance out at Mendoza, catching flies with the outfield. He's standing there with that old mitt of mine on, and he's sort of spraddled out and hunched forward like he's ready to break either way, like fielders do, and Briggs knocks him a soft fly ball and Mendoza breaks exactly the wrong direction and he can't turn back in time, and it drops and bounces to a stop before he gets there. He pounces on it with all two hundred twenty pounds and throws, and the ball bounces twice before it rolls past Briggs, twenty feet away.

Coach calls us in for a scrimmage and I'm catching behind the plate, and while I'm buckling on the chest protector, Mendoza walks past.

"Hey," I say quietly, "lighten up, man. Just do like we practiced. Pick it up and aim at the numbers and throw. No big deal."

He nods and trots out to right field and I see his mouth moving, and he's saying quietly to himself, "Aim at the numbers and throw. No big deal."

I jerk the mask down into position and squat behind the plate, and we start, and Ned does pretty good. Third batter bloops one out to Mendoza and he breaks the wrong direction and panics, and scrambles to pick it up, and throws and misses his cutoff man ten feet. I walk out in front of the plate and stand there while the ball comes back to Ned, and Mendoza's head is down and he's working with the mitt and I can tell he doesn't want to look at anyone, but I wait until he looks at me.

I point at my chest, and he knows. Aim for the numbers.

Three batters later Denny comes up and he hits a high one out to right field and it's going to come down right smack on Mendoza's head, and I think, this one he doesn't have to run for, this one he'll get.

The idiot starts to run to his right!

"No," I holler, "look at the ball."

He nearly gets back before it hits the ground. He pounces again and then I see him slow down, and his lips are moving, and I know what he's saying. Aim for the numbers.

He does. He stops dead still, looks at Jackie on second, studies the numbers on his chest, takes careful aim, and throws. It misses the numbers by five feet, but Jackie can get it. The only problem is, any runner in the league would have been past home plate and sitting on the bench while Mendoza was working it all out between his mind and his throwing arm.

I jerk the mask back into place and shake my head and round my cheeks while I blow air.

At the end of practice coach calls us around.

"We play the Cardinals in two days. No practice tomorrow. Be here at four thirty for the game."

We sack the equipment and toss it in coach's pickup, and he turns to me.

"Check to see what's wrong with Bernie, will you?"

I nod. "Sure."

"And you might tell him to think about playing catcher a lit-tle. We need backup for Ned."

I'm picking up my bike when Mendoza walks past. "Hey," I say to him, "you did okay out there."

His eyes show his pain. "Naw, bad."

"Quit worrying," I say, "and be here tomorrow at four. We'll throw a few."

"Okay," Mendoza says, and I can see the relief.

Stone picks up his bike down by the dumpster and I pedal over to him.

"Where does Bernie live," I ask.

"Up in the north end," he says. "Bradwell Street, I think."

"One of those monster homes?"

"Hotel," he says.

"What house number on Bradwell?"

"Forget the number. It's the biggest one and it's white and looks like a castle in Spain or Germany, or wherever they have those castles."

"Old?"

"New."

"Thanks." I start to pedal away when Stone stops me.

"Going to see Bernie," Stone asks, his nose wrinkled.

"Coach says find out why he wasn't here."

"You going to come down and throw some tomorrow?"

"Maybe."

"Cinnamon rolls too?"

"Probably."

Stone peddles off one way while I head the other, for home. Our house is at the north end too, but we're in a subdivision. Three blocks north of us, and east a little, out of the subdivis-ion, there's a vacant building lot with about a million big rocks in it, and it's for sale for three hundred thousand dollars, just for the empty lot and a million rocks and a ton of weeds. The Geezer checked on it. It's a pretty big lot, but it's no acre, or anything like that. From there, going north there are no more vacant lots. There are about two hundred great big homes and some of them are worth three or four million bucks!

And smack in the middle of the whole mess is Bradwell Street.

I pedal up there, and I swear, some of those homes are bigger than the Holiday Inn we stayed in for a day when we moved to Clearmont. They got two swimming pools and double tennis courts and basketball courts, and fancy iron gates on wheels, and four car garages, and Dobermans, and burglar alarms all over the place.

I pedal up Bradwell and it doesn't take long to find the big white castle. It's three stories high, with a white iron fence ten feet tall. I stop at the gate and can't figure out how to get in, when a stone pillar at one end talks to me, and I jump half out of my pants.

"Whom did you wish to see," the pillar asks.

I look and there's no one there, and I'm trying to figure out how to talk to a stone pillar, when it asks again.

"Bernie," I blurt out, and a Rolls Royce drives by and the driver looks at me and I feel like an idiot standing out there talking to a stone pillar!

"Your name, please."

"Joe. Joe Russell. Bernie's on the baseball team."

There's a pause.

"You may come in."

Great! How? Pole vault?

Something at the post clicks and hums and the two ton iron gate rolls open on its sunken track.

I look inside and I feel like I'm a CIA agent heading into a meeting with the mafia, like I saw in the movies. I grab my bike and walk on through, up a curved driveway made of bricks with flowers in the design, on up to the castle with four columns holding the roof three stories up. The chandelier over the door must have two million pieces of cut glass.

Half the big, white door opens and this Godzilla size maid is standing there wearing an apron and cap and a real hard look.

"You wanted to see Master Billman?"

"No. Bernie. I gotta talk to Bernie."

She frowns and her nose rises a little. "He's ill."

"Oh? Bad? Coach wants to know."

"He will recover."

"We got a game in two days. Coach wants him to catch. Can you tell him?"

I hear something move inside, and Bernie shows up behind this King Kong woman, and he's in a satin house coat and house slippers.

"Hi," he says.

The woman turns and points. "Back to your room, young man. Doctor's orders."

Bernie looks at her like she's got the measles. "I'm going to talk a minute." He walks right past her and she frumps around and walks away.

"Hi," I say. "You okay?"

He raises and drops his shoulders. "Okay."

"Coach was worried."

"I got a belly ache."

"Bad?"

"Naw. I guess too many hamburgers and cinnamon rolls."

I grin when I think about the contest last night. "Mendoza's okay," I say.

"When's the next game," he asks.

"Two days. Cardinals. Coach wants you to catch a little."

Bernie's eyes widen in surprise. "Me? Catch?"

"Yeah. Ned's going to pitch some. Mendoza's going to be right field backup."

Bernie shakes his head at the thought. "I'll be there for the game."

"Okay. No practice tomorrow, but some of us are going to be at the field at four to throw a few. Come on if you feel better. Get behind the plate and catch a few."

"You sure about this catching deal?"

"Coach said."

He shrugs again. "Okay. I'll be there tomorrow. Cinnamon rolls?"

"Maybe. I think mom's baking in the morning. Anyway, you got a bad stomach."

"It'll be better."

"See ya."

I turn to go and Bernie says, "You got the mask and chest thing? To catch?"

"No, but I think I can get it."

I turn to go again and he says, "Mendoza in right field?"

He's got a sick look on his face.

"Yeah. He'll be okay. Just needs to get out there and do it a couple times."

"Yeah, right," he says, and I see the doubt. I turn once more to go and again he stops me. "Who's coming tomorrow?"

And all of a sudden it hits me. Bernie hasn't got a friend in the world. He sits up here in this four million dollar pile of bricks and wears two hundred dollar satin bathrobes and rides around in limos and has trouble deciding which swimming pool to use today, and sees his mom and dad by appointment, and Druscilla The Terrible runs his life, and he's so starved for a friend he'd probably stand there all afternoon talking to me if I'd let him.

Something inside me turns over and I stop. "I don't know. Mendoza. Maybe Stone. Probably Webb and the Stotts. Just a bunch of us."

"Oh. Okay."

"Think you'll be there? I'll get the catching gear."

"Yeah. Maybe."

"Ever catch before?"

"Not serious. Just messing around."

"Know the signals?"

He just about freaks out. "No," he says real loud, and his eyes about bug out of his head he's so eager. "Do you?" I mean, he jumps on that so fast it jolts me.

"Sure."

"Show me!"

I look around. "Now?"

"Yeah. Come on in."

"You're sick. Druscilla won't like it."

"So what. Come on."

He leads me through an entry room big enough to play soccer, on down a hall so long the other end is hazy, and stops at his room.

Room? Cavern more like. The bed's a king double, and there's an olympic size sunken bathtub in the adjoining bathroom, and everything's immaculate and the best.

"Okay, show me," he says.

"Well, you got to squat down like you seen catchers do, and

you hide the signals between your legs."

"Like this?" He whips off the bathrobe and it hits a chair and falls to the floor, and he hunkers down.

I mean, when he drops into the catcher's position with those long tinker toy legs, he looks just like a giant grasshopper, and I swear those knobby knees are a foot above his head. But for the first time since I saw this guy, he's alive! That uppity look is gone. He's forgotten he's a rich doctor's pampered kid.

"Yeah," I tell him, "you got it. Okay. Here's the fastball sign." Index finger.

He practices.

"Right. Good. Here's curve." Two fingers

"Here's inside corner." Slant the fingers inside.

"Outside." Slant outside.

I show him all the signs, and he goes through them, and then I start firing him commands fast, like, fastball, curve, slider, inside, outside, and it starts to click, and I mean, Bernie's in another world.

"Okay," I say, "you got the idea. Come on out tomorrow if you're okay. We'll get the gear on you and see what you got."

I start back down that long hall and he's right there behind me.

"Hey, you gotta tell me which signs for which batters."

"You have to learn the batters. We'll start that tomorrow."

"Promise?" He's right there beside me, eyes wide and intent.

"Yeah. Be there."

Druscilla lets me out and the gate grinds open and I pedal on home.

Next day Mendoza's waiting for me, and I got an equipment bag over my shoulder with the catcher's gear and the cinnamon rolls. I lean it against the tree behind our bench, and signal to Mendoza to go on out in shallow right field. I stand at home plate and start knocking some of my old taped up balls out to him.

He misses the first four while I watch, because he's not following the ball when it leaves the bat. In the field, you got to see the ball leave the bat. It tells you almost all you need to know.

"Watch the ball when it leaves the bat," I call, "go the way it goes."

"Yeah," he calls back, and I smack another one. It's pretty high and easy, and about ten feet to his left. He waits and then starts to run, and doesn't get there in time.

"Start quicker," I yell, and smack another one, and this time he starts earlier and nearly makes it.

"Good. Great."

Next one, he gets a fair jump on it and he's there when it comes down, but he misses.

"Get your mitt out where you can see it. Up by your face."

The next one, he gets his mitt up by his face, and sure enough, the ball smacks his face, not the mitt.

"Sorry," he yells, and he's right, because he's going to have a black eye.

Stone wheels his bike in, and trots out to second to be the relay man for Mendoza, and Ned shows up and stands around for a minute, and then the Stotts drop their bikes and stand behind the backstop and Denny watches for a minute and then comes out behind the plate to take Stone's relay throws.

The sound of a motorbike turns us all towards the parking lot, and there's Bernie. He trots over and he's all smiles and eagerness. I dump the catcher's gear out of the big bag, and shove the cinnamon rolls sack back in, and Bernie starts buckling on the shin guards.

"Okay," I say to the other guys, "coach wants Bernie to catch a few and Jimmy to throw some. Mendoza, why don't you stand at the plate with the bat, and you other guys take the infield and we'll see what happens. Ned, we'll rotate at the mound."

Mendoza reluctantly steps up to the plate and Bernie drops down into that grasshopper crouch of his, and the other guys scatter around the infield.

"Mendoza, I'll throw easy and you watch until the ball hits the bat. Okay?"

He nods.

"Bernie, start the signals."

Index finger.

I wind up and let go an easy one. Mendoza swings and misses and Bernie's got his eyes closed because of the swing, and he misses too.

I wait for the next signal and it doesn't come because Bernie's forgot.

"What's my next signal," I call.

"Oh. Yeah. Sorry," Bernie says, and signals a curve.

I deliver a big, slow, looping curve. Mendoza doesn't swing, and Bernie catches it. I can see his keyboard through the mask.

I hand the ball to Ned and he throws a few, and we keep at it and pretty soon Bernie's giving inside-outside signals along with the regular stuff. Mendoza misses a lot and then he hits a few, and me and Ned keep it all slow and easy, and pretty soon Mendoza's hitting over half of them.

"Let's go for real," Bernie says, and Denny trots to the plate and Mendoza goes to the infield. I signal Bernie for a conference on the mound with me and Ned.

"Denny likes belt high fastballs over the outside of the plate. So what's your signal?"

Bernie thinks. "Curve, inside."

He goes back and squats and signs, and I deliver a big looping inside curve, and Denny swings and misses and Bernie nearly stands on his head trying to dig it out of the dirt and he misses.

"Go again," he calls and I wind up and deliver another one and Denny let's it go, and Bernie gets down to this one and I can see his keyboard through the mask.

We rotate through all the guys with me and Ned pitching for real, and Bernie's getting the hang of it really good.

"Okay, one more drill," I say. "No batter. Fastball, and you throw to second like a runner's stealing."

Denny trots to the second base and Ned cranks up and delivers. It whacks into Bernie's mitt and he comes out of his crouch throwing, and Ned forgets to get off the mound so Bernie's got a clear shot, and Bernie cocks to throw and then stops because he's afraid of hitting Ned.

"Hey," he hollers, and Ned turns to see what went wrong and then realizes he was supposed to get out of the way.

"Sorry," he says.

"It's okay," I cut in. "One more time."

Ned delivers and ducks away and Bernie fires, and his

throw is strong. A little high, but strong.

"Hey," I yell, "that's good."

"One more time," Bernie demands, and Ned cranks up one last fastball and again Bernie rifles it to second, and this time, I mean, that sucker's right on the money. Ankle high, right in front of the bag.

"Whoaaa," Ned hollers. "That's big league!"

Bernie jams his fist in the air and yells, "Yeahhhhhh."

We divide the cinnamon rolls and sit around in the grass and eat slow, and turn on the hose and pass it around, and there's some talk.

"How do you do your wrist when you throw a curve," Ned says.

I grab a ball and grip it and cock my wrist and say, "That's it. Rolls right over your finger. See?"

Bernie's watching close. "On that throw to second, is there a special way to grip?"

"Naw," Ned says, "no time. You just gotta grab it and throw."

"How about the mask? Do I get it off first?"

Ned shakes his head. "Naw, forget it. No time. It comes off anyway when you throw."

Bernie shoves his mouth full of cinnamon roll.

"Where was Chin?," Webb asks.

"Dunno," Denny answers. "Don't think he knew."

I turn to Mendoza. "Eye all right?"

It's a little puffy and he shrugs. "Okay."

"You done good on the batting."

"Naw, pretty bad."

"You're coming okay," I say. "Just keep working."

"Yeah," Bernie says, "work alone at home in front of a mirror."

Mendoza hasn't got a mirror or a bat, and with twelve kids at home hanging all over him, I doubt he ever has the time. I glance at him to see how he handles it.

"Good idea," is all he says.

Bernie says, "You were doing pretty good there at the last."

Mendoza glances at him and I see his eyes light up while Bernie's munching a cinnamon roll, and Bernie doesn't know what he's just done for Mendoza.

And for just a minute there, just a tiny second or two, the team had a feeling.

"Game tomorrow," Stone says and gets up, "I gotta get home."

"Yeah, me too," I say, and we load the catcher's gear and everybody heads for home.

At supper I turn to Mom. "You still team mother?"

"Yes." She passes the salad.

"Tomorrow Bernie catches, first time."

"That's nice," she says, and passes a baked potato.

"Be great if his Mom was there, or his dad."

Mom nods and passes the sour cream.

After we've cleared the table, I wait until I hear Mom on the kitchen phone and then I walk over by the archway to listen.

"Claire, this wonderful thing is going to happen tomorrow. I thought you should know."

There's a tiny pause.

"Bernie's going to catch a ball."

I cringe. He's going to play catcher, not catch a ball. He catches balls all the time. I blew it big time! Mom doesn't know catcher from outfielder.

"That's right! Catch a ball!"

Another pause.

"Well, no, not like all the other times. This time it's special!"

Another pause.

"I know, but I thought how nice it would be if you or your husband could be there."

I wait.

"He is? Oh, that's too bad. Perhaps you could find the time."

Another pause and this time it's a long one.

"Oh! Marvelous. I'll see you there. We can sit together."

I heave a sigh and relax. I don't know how, but she did it. Then I stop. See you there? Sit with Claire Billman? Mom with Claire Billman at a baseball game? That familiar knot twists my stomach into a pretzel, and I can hear it all ready. "KILL THE UMP," Mom bellows, and Claire quietly moves somewhere else in the bleachers, and that's the end of that.

"Geezer's going somewhere tomorrow?" I asked.

"San Diego. He might be back in time for the game, so I'll be there just in case."

My shoulders sag. "Mom, can you remember not to yell stuff? Like, kill the ump?"

Her eyebrows arch. "Isn't that what they say at baseball games? I heard it on tv."

"Not little league."

"I'll try to remember."

Next day I head for the field a little after four and the guys are starting to show up, and we get a surprise. The girl's league was given the north field for their game, and we got the south one. That means the sun is backwards from usual, and the field is slanted slightly south, so throws from the outfield will be easier, and out there about three hundred feet in right center field they got the steel poles for a soccer goal sticking up. We're all going to have to make some mental adjustments.

Stone and I start buckling the catcher's gear on Bernie, and he grins. "My Mom's coming today to watch."

"I know," I say, "and I think she's going to sit with my Mom. Your mom know anything about baseball?"

"I don't know," Bernie answers, "she's never said."

I'm just finishing the cross wrap on the shin guard strap when Bernie looks out at the parking lot.

"They're here," he says.

A white Cadillac a block long parks at the far end of the lot and my Mom and Claire Billman get out. Mom's wearing a nice looking skirt and blouse, but Claire Billman? She's wearing this knock out sky blue pants suit outfit and a white scarf, and a hairdo that cost at least two hundred bucks, and I stop and my eyes bug because I never seen anybody show up at a little league game looking like that.

Mom walks her over where we're working on Bernie.

"Are you ready for the game," she asks.

"Sure, Mom. Just helping Bernie." I glance up at Mrs. Billman. "Hi, Mrs. Billman."

"Hi," she says, real cool. "What's all this you're putting on Bernie?"

"His protectors."

"What for? Is this dangerous?"

"No, Mom," Bernie says, "this is what you wear when you catch."

She looks at him. "Are you afraid to catch?"

"No," my Mom interjects, "what he means is, that's what the boy wears who crouches down to help the umpire."

I glance up at Bernie and he's staring down at me with that "Who are these people?" look on his face.

Stone finishes with the chest protector and I give it a yank to be sure it's on good, and Bernie twists his hat backwards and slaps the backstrap of his mask behind his head, and perches the mask on the top of his head to walk out behind the plate.

"What's that for," his Mom asks, and points to the mask.

My Mom answers. "In case one comes down on top of his head."

"Oh," his mom says. "How thoughtful."

I walk Bernie out to the plate and glance at our Moms, seated in the second row right behind the plate. "Just stay cool," I say. "If I shake off your sign, just give me another one," and I walk on out to the mound.

We start our warmup, slow and easy, me throwing, Bernie catching, and the rest of the infield goes through their warmup with Chin throwing grounders and them fielding and throwing back, while Briggs hits fly balls to the outfield.

The Cardinals are over near their bench, standing around, waiting their turn, when Bernie and I hear his Mom.

"Are we winning?", she asks.

There's a pause. "I don't know," my Mom says, "I'm not sure they've started yet."

We trot off the field and the Cardinals go out and warm up, and the plate blue shoves a few baseballs in his belly pouch and calls us over.

"You know the rules. Cardinals' bat first. Let's play ball."

He slaps on his face mask and steps behind the plate. "Batter up," he calls, and the Cardinals' lead off hitter walks to the plate.

Bernie signs fast ball. This guy likes low fastballs and hates curves. I shake off the sign. Bernie signs slider and I shake it off. Bernie calls time and trots out to the mound.

"I forgot the sign for curve."

"Two fingers, and on this guy, inside."

Bernie grins and turns and trots back and crouches, and he signs curve, inside.

I nod slightly and he grins, and I crank up a looping inside curve, and this guy is swinging all the way and misses a mile. Bernie digs it out of the dirt and throws back.

I rub the ball a minute and then lean forward for the next sign.

Slider, outside. I nod and straighten and then I hear it from the bleachers. It's Bernie's Mom.

"I think Bernie has to go to the restroom."

I call time and signal Bernie out to the mound.

"You got to go to the restroom?," I ask.

"No," he says, and there's pain in his face. "She's picking up on the hand signals I'm giving down there."

I shrug.

"What's going on out there," the blue calls. "Come on, play ball."

Bernie trots back to the plate and drops into that grasshopper crouch and I deliver a slider and the guy misses, then a fastball a little high and inside and he gets enough of it to dribble it down to Stone, and Stone throws him out at first.

The next two go down swinging, and the top of the first inning is over. We trot to the bench and start unbuckling all the gear on Bernie because he bats fourth.

"Is the game over?," we hear from his Mom. "Who won?"

"No," my Mom answers, "our team bats before it's over."

"Oh. Do they put all those things back on Bernie?"

"I think so," my Mom answers, "later."

Our first two guys go down, then Chin hits a single, and Bernie comes up. Third pitch, he hits a blooper over the second baseman's head and starts for first, and it's going to be close. The second baseman gets to it, pivots too late to double Chin on second, and fires for first. Bernie beats it out by half a step, circles, and comes back to first.

"Was he supposed to hit it somewhere else," his Mom asks. "Why did he stop running?"

"I don't know," my Mom says, "I think he hit it all right."

Denny gets a single, and then Webb singles, and Bernie makes it home and trots to the bench and turns to grin at his Mom.

"Why didn't you run around again," his Mom calls, "you hit the ball in the right place."

There's laughter in the bleachers and Bernie stops grinning and turns back to the game.

At the end of the third inning, coach pulls me because he wants me to go the full seven innings on our next game, in two days. He puts Ned on the mound, and I take center field. Bernie stays at catcher. We're ahead, three to zip.

Ned has heart, and he gives it all he's got, but he hasn't had enough time to develop the tools. In the next two innings, he gives up five runs and they're ahead, five to three. The team has gone quiet, and we're sitting on the bench with long faces waiting for our bats in the top of the sixth.

Coach says, "Okay, Jackie take the mound, Ned on the bench, Mendoza, take right field."

We all look at the ground and then glance at Mendoza out of the corner of our eye, and take a deep breath. We know we're not going to win the second half of the season, but here we are in the sixth, down two runs, and he puts Mendoza in?

We go down without a run in the sixth, and silently take our positions in the field. I trot out with Mendoza to right field.

"Hey, just remember, watch the ball leave the bat. Stay cool. Throw for the numbers."

I see his lips moving. Watch. Throw for the numbers.

I leave him and take my position in center field, but I sag a lot towards him to back him up if I have to.

Jackie holds them in the sixth, and we don't score.

Top of the seventh, we take our bats with them still up two runs, five to three. We have to make three runs, and then Jackie's got to hold them in the bottom of the seventh.

Three runs.

I look around for the Geezer, but he's not there, and I wonder if he'll make it to see us lose this one. If we lose this first one, there's no chance for us this second half.

Our first batter is Chin and he is out at first on a dribbler to their second baseman.

Bernie is next, and this clown pulls a deal that nearly gets him killed by the team.

See, Bernie swings at the third pitch and connects solid. We watch this towering shot clear the center fielder's head and land past the soccer ball uprights out there three hundred feet in center field.

The whole team comes off the bench shouting, and Bernie cranks up all his tinker toys and starts around the bases.

With no fences out there, the center fielder turns and chases the ball, but we can see it's too far for him to get there and make the throw, so we're shouting, "Run Bernie Run" because this is a home run, and there's Bernie, knees and elbows going through their nutty gyrations while he streaks past second. He looks out to see what the center fielder is doing, and I see him hesitate just a little, and then he churns for third, and then this idiot slides!

I mean, center fielder has just picked up the ball and there's no way he's going to get it to home before Bernie gets there, and Bernie lays down on his right side and slides and hooks the bag.

Their third baseman's head drops forward and his mouth falls open because he can't believe it.

Coach is standing in the coach's box and he's shouting, "Run," and his arm's a windmill signalling Bernie on around third to home.

And there's Bernie, in the dirt, on his right side, in a perfect slide!

We leap off the bench in the dugout and slam into the chain link and all start screaming at the same time, "Run Bernie Run", and the coach is still shouting and windmilling.

Bernie gets to his knees with one hand on the bag, and signals the blue to call time, and the ump looks at him like he's lost his mind, and the blue doesn't call time because the ball is still in play.

Bernie thinks time is out and he stands up and dusts off his uniform, and he looks at the coach with a weird expression that says, "what's wrong with you?," and he puts his foot on third base and signals they can call time in whenever they're ready to play ball. The blue stands there in total confusion because he didn't call time out in the first place, and he's never seen anything so dumb in his whole life.

The center fielder cocks to throw, and he knows he's way too late to stop the home run, and then he sees Bernie go down in his slide, and his jaw drops clear to his knees when he sees Bernie stand up on third base and call time and start banging the dust out of his uniform.

His coach is standing near their bench shouting, and his team is jumping up and down in the infield screaming, "Throw the ball throw the ball" and the kid can't hear the words because by now both teams are nearly shouting in hysterics and the bleachers are into the act and the whole place is in an uproar.

The center fielder thinks something has gone wrong. Maybe somebody had a heart attack, maybe Bernie busted an ankle, maybe the blues called an ump's time out for some reason. He don't know what went wrong, so he starts to trot in with the ball in his mitt to find out what could cause a near riot.

He gets close to his second baseman, and the kid grabs the fielders arm and nearly pulls it off jerking the ball out of his mitt, and he rifles the ball to the catcher as hard as he can throw.

Bernie stands watching all this and listening to the uproar. He doesn't react until he sees the second baseman grab the ball from the center fielder and make the throw. Then Bernie takes off his batting helmet and scratches the top of his head for a minute and purses his mouth like he's thinking. Then he turns back towards us and he shrugs his shoulders and raises his eyebrows like he's surprised.

He doesn't say anything, just stands there and finally flashes his grin. He has just blown a homerun big time and he's trying to be as friendly as he can to keep us from killing him.

Coach signals for time and Ned signs to the blue and with time out, Coach and the whole bunch of us thunder out to third and surround Bernie to see what he can say to stop the murder.

Coach's face is a mask of pain. "What happened?"

Bernie clears his throat. "Well, I figured . . . when I came past second out there . . I seen their fielder . . . he's gesturing and doing all he can to slow down the end of his life . . . and I swear he had the ball and was ready to throw it on in to the relay man . . . and I figured it was going to be close . . . so I slid."

Coach throws his hands up in the air and his eyes roll into his head for a minute and the rest of us groan.

"Didn't you see me?," coach demands, "hear me?"

"Yeah, I did, but I couldn't figure out why you was sending me on home when the ball was coming in. You sure puzzled me."

Puzzle him? How about kill him?

Coach's shoulders droop and all the air goes out of him and I feel for the guy. The team turns away and starts back for the bench, mumbling to themselves, and then Bernie calls to us.

"Anyway, it was a pretty good hit, wasn't it?"

We all stop and turn back and Jimmy lays it on Bernie. "It wasn't the hit we're talking about, dork. It was the bonehead deal at third."

Bernie looks dejected and we go back to the bench.

Things go real quiet and then I hear it from the bleachers behind.

"Beautiful, Bernie, beautiful," my Mom's calling.

His Mom stands up and claps. "Good playing, son, you nearly got a touchdown."

There's a titter in the bleachers and it grows to two minutes of loud guffaws, and there's Mom and Mrs. Billman, beaming, clapping, congratulating each other and thanking all the fans for their support.

I shake my head in pure misery.

So there we are. Bottom of the seventh, one out, Bernie on third, and Denny comes to bat.

After him, Mendoza, and after Mendoza, it is me.

Denny has to do two things. He has to hit safely and he has to get Bernie home.

He chips a little dribbler off between the mound and third base. Their third baseman stays at his base because Bernie is there and he has to hold him, so the pitcher has to charge off the mound and field the ball. Then he has to turn completely around and hit first base. He sets and hesitates just long enough to hold Bernie on third, and then turns and delivers but he's just a hair late. Denny gets there half a step ahead of the ball.

Denny is on first, Bernie on third, and we have one out.

Mendoza's turn.

I see the sweat on his lip and the blank look in those dark eyes as he sorts through the bats for the lightest one.

"Hey, easy, just meet the ball. No big deal."

He tries to say something but his voice won't work and he walks out to the batter's box, and you can almost hear the snickering among the other team's infield.

Mendoza takes two called strikes without moving a muscle, and then on the last pitch he closes his eyes and swings. The problem is, their pitcher is way ahead of him and the pitch is eight inches outside. Mendoza couldn't have reached it no matter what.

He walks away from the batter's box with his head down, and I pass him.

"Next time," is all I say, and he just keeps walking.

I walk to the box and get my head working. Two outs, men at first and third, down two runs. We got to get three. I got to get a hit, and hope Randy, who follows me, can get a hit too.

I smooth the dirt with my cleats and settle in and it starts through my mind. Keep your head down, eye on the ball, swing level, just meet it, pull with your left push with your right, just meet it. The power will come if you just swing smooth and meet it.

First pitch. The very first pitch. "Tank."

I can't believe it. It's Bernie's hit all over again. The ball clears the center fielder's head and drops between the uprights clear out in the soccer field and rolls.

This time the coach ROARS. "BERNIE, RUN." Bernie breaks for home and Denny is past third when I round first base. I pass second looking to see where the center fielder is and he hasn't reached the ball yet.

I round second and lock onto the coach to get my signal whether I should go on home because I can't take the time to look out in center field to see where the ball is. Coach is motionless until I'm twenty feet from the base and then his arm starts to windmill and he shouts "Run" and I round third churning.

Coming in to home plate I don't know where the ball is so I slide and their catcher is blocking the plate and I take him out and hook the plate with my toe just as the ball comes sailing over the top of both of us and rattles into the backstop.

Three runs! Six to five, our favor! The team is behind the chain link jumping around like idiots and shouting, and coach comes running, and I trot around to the bench and the team mobs me.

Things settle and out of the corner of my eye I see the Geezer and I turn my head to look.

He's standing there pretty sober, and then he nods his head and I see a little smile. Why couldn't he just once run over and tell me I did good and maybe even put his arm around my shoulder?

I turn back to the team. "This aint over 'til it's over. They got three more outs. We got to hold 'em."

Randy hits to the shortstop and is thrown out at first and the top of the seventh is in the books, finished.

Jackie takes the mound and Coach pulls Ned in to catch, and Bernie goes to the outfield with me and Mendoza. I sag over as far as I dare towards Mendoza to back him up.

First batter pops out.

Jackie gets ahead of the second batter, but on his third pitch he hits the guy's wrist just enough, and the blue sends the batter on down to first.

Next batter drives one right back over second base and they got two on base, one out.

Next batter hits a long fly straight out to Bernie and he takes it on the run and throws it back to the relay man, but both batters have tagged and they both move up one base, second and third.

Two down, runners on second and third, we're still up by one.

Next batter settles in and Jackie takes a big breath, then goes into his windup.

It is a high fly ball to shallow right field.

Mendoza!

I sprint at the crack of the bat and watch the ball arching, and it's going to land about twenty feet in front of Mendoza, but he hasn't moved, and I shout at him, "Run," and he finally starts but too slow, and I'm coming down on him and the ball like a tornado, and the ball bounces six feet in front of him and I bare hand it right off the grass and load and fire for home.

The runner on third saw all this developing, and he's back on third tagged up in case Mendoza catches the ball, but when he sees Mendoza can't get there, he starts for home.

What he didn't see was me coming from Mendoza's right, and what he didn't know was about my arm.

My shot for home plate passes about four feet over Chin's head like a bullet, and it settles just enough to hit Ned dead center, and Ned takes it whacking into his mitt, and drops to both knees as the runner starts his slide, and the runner slams into Ned and there's a big cloud of dust at the plate and arms and legs sticking out, and then Ned scrambles up and holds the ball high in his left hand.

"Yer out," the blue yells, and it's over!

We did it! The team comes thundering in from the field and swarm Ned at the plate, and then me, and they're jumping around like they've lost their minds until the coach settles them down, and we line up for high fives with the Cardinals.

I hear Claire Billman's voice, and it's high and excited. "Aren't they going to arrest that one boy? Why, the very idea, running into that other boy and knocking him down right there in front of us! It's criminal!"

My Mom says, "I think he's supposed to do that."

Mrs. Billman slaps her hand over her mouth in shock, and then says, "Why, the very idea! Who won?"

"I think we did," Mom says.

"Oh. Well, that's different."

Ned looks at her, and then at me, and then at Bernie, like, where's she from?

We sack up the gear, and the Geezer helps with the catcher's gear.

"Nice throw," he says. "Nice hit, too." He keeps working the gear into the bag.

That's all I get from him. Old, out of it, ho hum, - the Geezer. I feel it and I just have to swallow the feelings inside and forget how cool it would be if he would just once, just once, cut loose and be crazy when I do it right.

12

CHIN TAKES ON A BLUE

"WE GOT A TOUGH WEEK," coach says. "We play the A's on Thursday and the Blue Jays on Friday, back to back. Joe and Ned start against the A's, and Jackie and Bernie start against the Blue Jays."

Thursday, I spend half an hour before the game, thinking over the A's. They were pretty tough in the first half, and they got a couple of dangerous hitters. I pedal on down to the field a little early and take my time putting on my cleats.

The guys trickle in, and the A's gather over on their bench, and after warmups, the blue gathers us at home plate for the usual instructions. We're home team and he doesn't waste time. He pulls his mask down and walks to the plate.

"Batter up," the blue calls, and we trot out to the field.

People who watch tv baseball think most pitchers are like zombies, because they don't change expression, no matter what. Nine strikeouts or nine homeruns, they got the same look on their face.

What the tv watchers don't know is that if you are going to handle the pressure on the mound, you got to learn to shut out the world and concentrate on one single thing: nail the batter. And that means you got to concentrate so hard you don't see, nor hear, nor think anything else. Homerun or strikeout, you got to take it all and stay cool, in control, no emotion, straight face.

By the third inning we're all aware this game has turned into a pitching duel between me and their pitcher, a rubber armed kid named Ryals. I'm putting their guys down one, two, three, and he's doing the same to us. End of the fifth, we're tied at zip.

In the sixth I miss the inside corner of the plate about half an inch and the blue calls "Ball" and I give them the only walk they're going to get. They got a man on base.

Next pitch gets away from Ned and the guy on first steals second.

Next batter hits a dribbler out to second base and the runner advances to third on a fielders choice and there is one out.

The next batter goes down on strikes and now they got a man on third with two out, and this is their first real threat in the whole game.

I rub the ball a little and I think about their batter. Good hand-eye coordination, no power, but he hits about .380 and gets a lot of singles. He likes the ball a little high and right down the middle. If he singles, the guy on third scores.

Ned signs curve. I deliver and the curve arches in just about where he likes it for height, but on the outside edge of the plate where he can't hit it solid. He passes it and takes a called strike.

Ned signs sinker.

I blow an inside sinker past him for a called strike two and I'm ahead of him, two strikes, no balls.

I waste a curve high and inside to dust him off the plate and he pulls back.

Next I repeat the sinker on the outside edge and he swings because he has to, and taps one right back to me and I throw him out at first and the threat is over.

Bottom of the sixth, I bat first and I go out on a pop fly in foul territory over by third base.

Webb follows me and beats out a weak hit right down first base line and is on first safe.

One out, one man on first. Stone comes up and they sag their infield back just a little and the pitcher throws him a nice, fat, slow one right down the middle. They figure to let him hit and try for the double play.

Stone hits to the infield all right, but Webb is way ahead of them and he's running before Stone swings. Their second baseman fields, turns to look and knows he can't beat Webb at second, and throws just in time to get Stone at first.

Two out, Webb on second.

Now this crazy, unbelievable thing happens.

Their center fielder wears goggles. I never did know why because they aren't the kind that improves your vision. They just sit there and keep the rain out, I guess, and we haven't seen rain the whole season and there is sure no rain this afternoon. I figure the guy just thinks they look cool.

So anyway, he takes off his hat and yells, and signs for time, and the blue thinks he has an equipment problem, so he calls time. Then this guy takes off his goggles and pulls a handkerchief out of his back pocket and starts to clean them. He blows on them and rubs them, and then holds them up to the sun and looks through them and blows on them some more, and dabs at them a time or two.

We're all standing around and pretty soon I get the picture. This Broadway class production is to make us wait, to give us a message. "You will wait until I am ready. You will play when I say so." He figures to get us antsy, off balance.

Webb's got this sour look on his face at second, and he tugs at his pants and looks disgusted, and the blue is out of patience by this time and he yells, "Play ball."

Ned steps up to the plate and sets to hit, and the pitcher delays just a minute while this guy out there in center field settles his goggles into place, and then the pitcher starts his wind up while the guy puts his hat back on, and then the pitcher delivers.

While the ball is on its way to the plate we all hear this whining sound in center field like a jet engine winding up, and Ned whacks a good, solid line drive out over second base and it bounces strong on its way right to this guy in center field.

Forget the baseball.

When the ball hits the ground on the first bounce we hear this sound like a werewolf during full moon and every eye in

Griffith Park whips onto this center fielder.

He throws his mitt thirty feet in the air. His arms are gyrating so fast they are blurry, first above his head and then on his head then out at his sides, then back above his head again. His feet are hitting the ground at three thousand rpm's and his werewolf sound has changed to a high mountain elk mating call. Then a wounded water buffalo. Then several hyenas.

He throws himself on the ground and bounces right back up and his feet are still hitting the ground at three thousand rpm's and he finally whips his hat off and jerks the goggles off and throws them into the grass and claps his hands over both eyes.

He hits the ground again and this time he lays there for a minute and then he gets onto his knees and sounds like the jet plane again and topples over backwards moaning with both hands still over his eyes.

When Webb hears all this stuff in the outfield, and looks out at this guy doing acrobatics no human ever did before, he's absolutely entranced. The ball rolls out within ten feet of this guy while he is going through his routine, and Webb just stands there like he's hypnotized.

Coach cups his hands and shouts "WEBB."

Webb shakes his head and seems to wake up just as Ned comes steaming in to second base and Webb breaks for third, Ned right behind him.

They both round third and go on to home and cross the plate five feet apart. We're up, two to zip.

The blue calls an umpire's time out and the coach from the other team runs out to this guy in center field and the whole A's team goes with him, and our coach and team are right behind them.

The fielder is still rolling around moaning and his coach drops to one knee and grabs his arms. His hands are still covering his eyes.

"What happened, what's wrong," their coach yells. None of us can see anything to explain what made this guy go nuts.

More moaning.

"Where does it hurt?," their coach demands.

The guy stops his moaning long enough to speak. "Don't know - a flying monster - my goggles."

Every eye turns up to the sky looking for one of those monster prehistoric birds with the big beak and the long pointy tail that flies off carrying dinosaurs. Nothing up there but a few seagulls and ravens.

Then all eyes go to his goggles. His coach wrinkles his forehead and thinks for a minute and picks them up. When he does, those of us nearest the coach see it.

A bee crawls out of one of the eye covers and onto the elastic head band, and stops for a minute before it flies away towards the dandelions.

Everybody on both teams falls into hysterics. Their coach sobers long enough to be sure the bee didn't sting the kids eye, and then he's laughing again, so hard he has tears.

Five minutes later the blue quits laughing and yells "Play ball" and both teams quit rolling on the ground and try to control their laughter for the rest of the game.

The batters on both teams stand there at the plate trying to be serious when they are batting, and then they bust out laughing and the pitcher throws and nobody even swings. Both teams go down, one two three, all on called strikes.

The game ends, two to zip, our favor.

Baseball is like life. Who would ever think we would win a game because some idiot on the other team gets a bee inside his goggles? And if you're the A's, who would ever think you'd lose for the same reason?

We got no time to practice before we play the Blue Jays the next day. We show up ahead of time for the game, and while we're warming up for the A's, I get another one of Mom's surprises.

The aircraft carrier pulls into the parking lot and Ming Chin gets out. She's wearing a blue silk dress and looks like a China doll. Mom waves and calls, and Ming waves and hurries over to sit beside Mom, and Claire Billman.

Somewhere in the back of my mind I see those three monkeys, see no evil, hear no evil, speak no evil. I wonder what "KILL THE UMP" sounds like in Chinese. I look at Chin and he looks back at me and the expression on his face never changes, but his eyes do. He is as surprised as I am.

There is no time to worry about it because the blue calls us to the plate, gives the standard instructions, pulls his mask down and hollers, "Play ball."

Jackie's on the mound and Bernie's catching. I'm in center field.

The Blue Jays have lost half their games in this part of the season, and they're not contenders for the championship, but they're really up for this game because the only claim they might have to glory in the whole season is beating us - the team who won the first half.

Things go fast through the first three innings, and at the top of the fourth we're tied at one run each. They're starting to believe they might win. We can see it in their faces, and the way they're taking chances and starting to yell things at us to psyche us out.

There's this short, husky kid with long black hair that hangs to his shoulders and sticks out like a bush under his hat. He only has one eyebrow that reaches across both eyes, and looks like he's been shaving since he was six. He gets real mouthy yelling at our infield and finally gets around to Chin.

"Go back to China," he yells.

Chin glances at him and shrugs it off.

Fifth inning, the guy picks it up again. "Miss your rice this morning?," the guy yells and laughs.

Webb looks pained, and yells at this guy, "You got a problem?"

The guy comes off his bench and rattles the chain link. "Naw, but your first baseman's busted his chopsticks." He laughs real loud, like somehow that's the joke of the year.

Chin pulls his dictionary out of his hip pocket and looks up a word and shakes his head and jams the book back in his pocket.

The Blue Jay coach sits the guy down and we move on.

Sixth inning we score two runs, and we're up three to one, and they come to bat. Jackie gets the first batter, but he's getting tired, and coach pulls Ned in to pitch. Ned gets the next guy on a grounder to second, and then this husky loud mouth picks up his bat and comes to the plate.

Ned gets ahead of him, one ball, two strikes, then moves him back with an inside fastball, and then he puts one right down the middle, just a little high, and the guy hits a grounder out to

Stone at third. Stone fields it smooth and loads to fire but he bobbles it just a little and recovers and fires to Chin.

This loud mouth sees the ball coming and he knows it's going to get to Chin just about the same time he hits first base. Chin's standing clear off the bag, towards second and he's got his left foot jammed against the the side of the base, just like he should. This guy sees all this and with his last two steps he cuts just slightly to his left and hits first base with his left foot, clear over on the left edge, and he makes sure he gets a piece of Chin's foot when he does it.

The ball hits Chin's glove just as the guy's foot comes down on Chin's foot, and I see Chin wince from the pain, and he jerks his foot away and drops to his knee and grabs his ankle with both hands, and the ball rolls away. His jaw is set real hard but he doesn't make a sound. He just hunches there on one knee holding his ankle.

I call time and run over, and coach comes running, and Webb comes tearing over. This guy is standing off to one side and he's wearing this real ugly smile. The coach pulls down Chin's stirrup and stocking, and you can see the cleat marks, and bad bruises. The blue shakes his head.

Denny walks right up to this mouthy guy and yells, "You done that on purpose."

The guy smirks. "He was blockin' the bag."

"Naw," Denny says, "you done it on purpose."

Now the guy's face changes from this smirky grin to real ugly, and he says, "Prove it."

Denny jerks off his mitt and throws it in the dirt and faces the guy, and he goes nose to nose, and he shouts, "What do you say we go a round or two," and he raises his hands, ready to fight, and he starts straight into this guy.

Coach grabs Denny and pulls him back, and the other coach grabs the mouthy guy, and the blue steps into the middle of it.

"I'm going to have to put him out of the game," he says, and points to Denny.

Chin grabs his book and looks up a couple of words, then turns to the blue. "Not right," he says, and points to the mouthy guy. "Him."

The blue doesn't understand Chin's accent, and shakes his

143

head.

"You're out of here," he says to Denny, and points.

Chin hobbles over to the blue on his bare foot and again points and says, "Not right. Him." He points to the other guy.

The blue looks at coach. "I don't understand what he's saying."

Coach says, "He's from Taiwan. Let's play ball."

The blue nods and jerks his thumb and Denny's out of the game.

And that's when Chin comes unglued. He jerks out his book and he thumbs for words and he can't find them fast enough, and he rips off about thirty seconds of pure Taiwanese.

For the first time, the expression on his face changes. I mean, Chin comes on like a warrior. He doesn't even look at his book, but tears of another thirty second speech at the blue, in Taiwanese, and I mean, from the sound of his voice, he's a born Kamikaze.

The blue stops and turns back.

"What's he saying," he says. "Is he disagreeing with me?"

By now the whole team's gathered out there on the grass between first base and the mound, not knowing what to do. Up in the bleachers I hear this shrill voice that sounds just like Chin, and there's Ming, shaking her fist and making a statement that sounds like what Chin just said.

Chin faces the blue and now he's waving his hands, and he dumps another load of Taiwanese on the blue.

"One more time," the blue says to coach, "I'm going to throw him out too."

Chin doesn't know what the blue said, but he does know Denny's still out of the game, and he knows this is all coming out wrong, and he spews all over the blue one more time.

"He's outta here," the blue says.

We're all standing there looking at each other, not knowing what to say or do, when Randy takes charge. He runs to Chin and grabs the book out of Chin's back pocket and opens it and fumbles in it for a minute and says to the blue, "All he did was agree with you. I got it right here."

"He agreed with me?"

"Yeah. Right here." Randy puts his finger on a page. I'm

standing right there and I glance at it.

The blue looks skeptical, so Randy jams the book into Chin's hands. Chin catches the idea and quickly finds a page in the Chinese section, and points to a Chinese symbol, and Randy looks at it, and I'm looking over his shoulder. Beside the Chinese symbol is the English word, "Stupid."

"He says you're smart," Randy says, and points. He shoves the book back to Chin, who finds another Chinese symbol and again Randy reads it with me looking over his shoulder. The English word is "Idiot."

"He says you were right." Randy points and pushes the book back to Chin, who finds the next one and I read it with Randy. "Moron."

Randy nods. "He says you made the right call."

"You sure about all this," the blue says, with doubt written all over his face.

"It's right here," Randy says, and closes the book and hands it to the blue. The blue leafs through a few pages, then hands it back to Randy.

"Let's play ball."

Coach turns to Chin. "Okay? You play?"

Chin gets enough to understand. He nods his head, and puts his stocking and stirrup and shoe back on.

I'm standing there holding my breath, afraid the blue will get suspicious about how Randy blew it past him, but he doesn't, and I look at Randy wide eyed, and he raises his eyebrows.

"Sometimes you gotta do things," he says to me quietly, and trots on over to third base.

Chin limps a little on his way back to first base. Coach shifts Denny in to cover second, and Mendoza takes right field.

Next batter drives a hard one bouncer to Randy, and Randy throws to Denny on second, who relays on over to Chin at first to turn the double play, and the game ends three to one, our favor.

We're loading the equipment before I start to laugh at how Randy smoked that blue with Chin's Chinese book. Randy's over gathering up the bats and he looks at me funny.

I look at him and I'm still laughing. I don't say anything, but he catches on, and then he starts to laugh too. Pretty soon we're standing there laughing at each other and some of the guys ask what's so funny, but Randy and me don't say a word. I don't think anyone ever knew why, except the two of us.

I'm on the way home before another thought hits me, and I sober up.

We're half way through the second part of the season, and we haven't lost yet. We got the Angels next, and then the Cubs, and last, the Orioles. The Angels are the only team that beat us the first half, and the Cubs are coming on tough right now, and the Orioles haven't been beaten yet this half either.

And the Orioles have put out the word. This half, we're dead meat, and they plan to barbecue us.

13

THE ANGELS. THE ONLY TEAM that beat us in the first half of the season, and they did it on Leo Perry's hit. Nobody says anything, but there's a quiet feeling that this half, we get these guys. I can feel it while we're warming up before the game.

The blue pulls his mask down and calls, "Play ball."

We bat first, and I look out at their infield, and I can see it in their faces - they mean to win this one. Their pitcher is Conkel, and he's pretty good. Not too fast, but mixes up his pitches and he can beat you if you aren't careful.

Ned steps into the batters box and kicks a hole for his back foot and faces the first pitch. He whacks an easy grounder and is thrown out, Randy gets to first on a single, Chin goes out on a pop fly and Bernie brings Randy home for our first run on a long double down the first base line. Denny goes down on strikes.

Top of the first inning is over and we have one run.

We trot out onto the field and I rub the ball and take a look at their first batter.

I blow three past him and he's out, and the next batter grounds out to Webb. The third batter takes two called strikes, and then I see a sort of controlled rage in his eyes. Ned signs sinker, and the ball drops about a foot and he misses it a country mile. I mean, he intended to cream that thing.

Second inning, Webb takes first on a walk, and I bring him home with a double, and our next two guys go down in order. Score, two to zip.

Bottom of the second, Ned pulls his mask down and the blue calls for a batter and we go.

Conkel is first. He doesn't have power but he has speed, and hits a lot of singles. I strike him out on five pitches, and while I'm rubbing the ball, Leo comes to the plate.

I look, and he takes his stance, and he and I have a little sort of unspoken duel going on. He's their best hitter.

Ned signs curve outside, I shake it off, and then Ned signs fastball. I put one on the outside corner, just below the letters, and Leo lets it go for a called strike.

Next fastball moves him back about a step and is a called ball.

Ned signs for a curve, but I shake it off again. It was a curve Leo hit the first half, that got us in trouble. Ned signs sinker.

The ball drops about 8 inches and Leo swings from the heels and misses. Strike two.

Ned signs curve again, and I think that one over, and I nod and we go. I see Leo knows what's coming, and it's sort of like, "Okay, friend, let's see if you can blow it past me."

And I do. The curve comes in shoulder high and then breaks down and away, and Leo starts his swing. When the ball's just above his knees it catches the corner of the plate, and Leo tries to correct his swing and can't, and he's called out on strikes.

Their next batter bounces a soft one right back to me and he's out on first.

Next inning both sides go down, one, two three. We're still ahead two to nothing, and they're starting to get tense because they've been through their batting order and haven't got a hit yet.

From our dugout we see their coach call them to a huddle in their dugout and they're dead quiet while he draws diagrams on a clipboard and we wonder what kind of super strategy they're cooking up. The blue calls for a batter and we don't have time to worry about it.

Top half of the fourth, we leave two stranded again before

we're retired, and we go into the bottom half.

They come to bat and we're silent, watching for the super strategy their coach wrote on the clipboard.

First batter is their catcher and he is a long ball hitter. He takes a fastball strike, and then I see him study his coach for a minute, and I got an idea what that was about, and I deliver a slow curve.

He squares to bunt, which is what I figured his coach wrote on the clipboard, and I'm moving to the first base line before he makes contact. I bare hand it to Chin and this guy's out. I see him grinding his teeth and muttering on the way back to the dugout.

Their next batter steps into the box, and there's something about the way he's standing. I call time and walk over to Stone. "Watch for a bunt down third," I say quietly and he moves back to his usual position.

The guy lays a bunt right down the line towards Stone, and Stone is running forward at the crack of the bat and nails the guy at first.

Their next batter comes to the plate and I read this guy like a book. Forget bunting - this guy intends putting the ball in the next county.

I dust him off with an inside curve and then I blow a fast ball past him.

I can see his face becoming redder by the second.

I deliver a sinker that drops out from under his swing and I'm ahead of him on a count of one ball, two strikes. I own him. A fastball smacks into Ned's glove while he's swinging, and he's out on strikes.

The fourth inning is over, and we can feel the tension coming from their bench.

I make a mistake in the bottom of the sixth and the batter swings with both eyes closed and smacks one in the hole over second, for their first hit, but we put the next three down in order and they don't score.

At the end of the sixth inning, we're still leading two to zip. I've put Leo down three times without a hit. The last time he looked at me and smiled, like, you done good, and I smiled back, like, you too.

Top of the seventh, Webb gets a single and I get a single, and we got men on first and second. Jackie hits into a double play that puts me and him out, but Webb goes on to third. Stone goes down on strikes, our last out, and the top half of the seventh is over.

We are still leading, two to zero.

Bottom of the seventh, the first pitch is a curve and Ned doesn't get his mitt low enough and misses it, and when he comes out of his crouch to go get it, he sort of stumbles and catches himself on his right hand and jams his thumb on the ground. He flinches and buckles over holding his hand against his chest protector.

For just a second I'm scared it's broken. The blue calls an umpires time and we all run up to see what Ned's done. The thumb is sore but he can flex it good so it isn't broken, but he can't control his throw with it.

Coach takes charge. "Ned, go to the bench and get ice on that right now. Bernie, you catch. Mendoza, you take right field. Webb, go to center."

The whole thing sort of unsettles us. You know, who would expect Ned to sprain a thumb, and we'd wind up with Bernie to finish the game behind the plate, and Mendoza out there in right field.

"Batter up," calls the blue and I take a look at their next batter.

Bernie signs fastball and this guy goes down in four pitches, called strikeout.

Their next batter gets their second hit, a dribbly little bouncer out over second base again, and they have a man on first.

Their third batter is a good contact hitter so I brush him back about six inches with a high inside fastball and then blow a curve past him. Next pitch is a sinker and he misses it. I'm ahead of him on a one ball two strike count.

I throw him a pretty fair fastball just a little high and inside but he swings, just like I knew he would, and makes contact. It pops about fifty feet in the air right to Stone, who catches it for the second out.

Their next batter is Conkel, and he's showing a lot of frustration because he's pitched a pretty good game, but he's losing.

Conkel is a pull hitter.

I move him back with a high inside pitch and he settles down for the next pitch.

He likes a fast ball just a little inside so he can pull it right down the third base line for extra bases.

The next pitch drops in, a heavy curve that is a called strike. Then, a sinker and he swings and tips it foul over Bernie's head and it bounces off the blue's chest protector.

One ball, two strikes.

I rub the ball and signal Bernie, and he calls time and trots out to me.

"Fast ball, outside. He'll tap a grounder to me."

Bernie trots back to the plate.

I deliver and Conkel swings.

He makes contact just like I figured, but he hits the ball nearly on the top, and drives it into the dirt right in front of home plate. Conkel throws the bat down in disgust and sprints for first base.

Bernie sees the swing and hears the contact, but with the mask on he can't see the ball on the ground for a second. Right then, he should have thrown the mask off so he could see what's going on, but he forgets. Then he tips his head forward and sees the ball and pounces.

And then this idiot gives us another cardiac attack with a Bernie Special.

He picks the ball up, and he loads to fire to Chin, and Conkel is half ways to first, digging dirt with every stride.

We're all standing like statues waiting for Bernie to throw to Chin.

Then the clown uncocks his arm and lowers the ball in front of the mask and I swear, he starts turning it, looking at it.

Everybody on the team screams, "Throw it, Bernie, THROW IT." The coach throws his hat on the ground, and bellows, "BERNIE, THROW IT!" All we can see in our mind is the last time Bernie pulled one of his mental lapses, and slid into third when he had a sure home run.

By now their coach and team are banging on the chain link in front of their bench shouting, "RUN CONKEL RUN," and their guy that was on first when Conkel hit the ball is past second, digging for third with all he's got and it's clear he doesn't intend stopping until he hits home base.

"THROW IT BERNIE" we're shouting, and suddenly Bernie raises his head and it seems like about an hour before he realizes where he is and what he's doing, and he cocks his arm and fires.

The ball smacks into Chin's glove one milisecond before Conkel's foot hits the bag. Conkel is out and the game is over, and we beat the Orioles, two to zip.

Forget the score, and forget the fact we only got two games left in the season and we might have a chance at the city championship. We all come tearing in to home plate to see what kind of brain kink Bernie had this time, and he's standing there all smiles, like, what's the big deal.

Ned's got his hand in an ice pack and he yells, "Bernie you idiot, why didn't you throw?"

"Oh, yeah, that," Bernie says, and flashes that killer smile of his. "You know," he starts, "I got the ball, and then the darndest thought hit me."

We're standing there with our mouths open, frozen, silent, waiting for Bernie to give us this big revelation about what thought could have cost us the game.

He looks serious. "I never knew who made them balls."

"What," Stone yells.

"Yeah," Bernie says. "So I figured I'd just take a second and read the trade mark."

Nine baseball mitts hit him at the same instant and he stands there in surprise. "Hey," he says, "what's the big deal? I got him didn't I."

Randy and Denny hit him with all the ice and water in the ice bucket and he's standing there on home plate dripping in a big puddle.

"Awright," Jackie says, "who makes 'em."

Bernie brightens. "Rawlings Cork Center," and he grins like he just delivered the news of the century.

"You dork," Webb says, "you mean Rawlings makes them and they got cork centers."

"Naw," Bernie says indignantly, "that aint what the trade mark said. It said, Rawlings Cork Center."

"Yeah, right," Jackie says.

"Well," Bernie says defensively, "you guys was yelling and I didn't have time to read it good. What do you expect?"

Coach gets us back under control and we line up for the usual high five exchange with the Angels, and Bernie has to go through the line dripping. I mean, those Angels are a pretty grim bunch. They meant to beat us the second half, just like they did in the first. Leo stops me after it's over and grins.

"Great game."

"You too," I say.

I ride home with the Geezer, and he's humming one of his little ditties, and after a block or two, he starts to talk. Not about how we beat the Angels, or that we played a good game, or even about Bernie. No, I get it again.

"Batting average's come up," he says.

"Yeah," I say.

"Batting .315," he says. "After supper, get out the batting tee and go through fundamental drills some more before the next game."

"Yeah, I'll do that." I wonder how it would feel if he'd just say, great game, good job, and let it go at that.

Two more games.

After supper I get out the batting tee.

14

THAT BIG HOTSHOT BOZO that slid third and took Stone out in the first half of the season plays for the Cubs, and I'm waiting for him. He comes to bat three times, and two times I strike him out, and the third time he smacks a line drive that's smoking, right to Stone, and Stone takes it and does his helicopter routine and the guy's out. He doesn't reach first base once in the entire game, and that's the best way I know to keep a bully from hurting guys sliding into a base. Just keep him off the bases.

We win the game five to one, but forget that we won, and forget that we took that big hero clear out of the game. We couldn't remember the score or that bozo ten minutes after the game ended, and we didn't stop laughing until the next day.

See, the coach of the Cubs is that pear shaped guy with the hair that sticks out of his baseball cap, Will Shellins. His kid, Harry Shellins, plays on his team. Harry is a slender kid, maybe just under six feet tall, and he is sort of academic. I mean, not like he's a super student or anything, but he always dresses neat and he is sort of quiet and acts like a gentleman. You know, academic.

His dad's trained him in baseball pretty good and he does a fair job as a fielder, and sort of ho hum with the bat. Good form, and makes contact with the ball, but he gets thrown out at first a lot because he has no power, and he runs nutty.

About his running, Harry has this one thing. When he runs, somehow his feet seem to hit the ground too far in front of him, and it looks like he's always trying to catch up with his feet. And when they hit the ground, they make this "plop plop plop" sound, like tennis rackets hitting the ground on their flat side. And he runs pretty slow.

So in the sixth inning he gets on base on a single and advances to third on a double by the next batter. There he is, waiting on third for someone to get a hit and bring him home.

Next batter goes down on strikes, and their next batter comes to the plate.

He gets a good, solid single into right field.

Harry starts for home. Plop plop plop.

We watch Jackie out in right field get the ball and we know he will be too late to nail Harry at home plate.

Plop plop. Harry is just about ten feet from home plate when all of a sudden he grabs his lower stomach and doubles over and flops right down on his belly on the base path and starts rolling back and forth, moaning and groaning and his knees are buckled up into his chest and his hands shift down and start holding the lower part of his stomach.

We leap off the bench and jam our noses through the chain link to see what got him, and we can't see a thing. Maybe a heart attack, but a guy doesn't grab his lower stomach when he's had a heart attack, and besides, what kid fourteen has a heart attack? Maybe an appendix attack. But we don't think that's how they happen.

His Dad, the coach, is over behind the chain link, in front of their bench, and his head jerks forward and he watches all this for a second, and we're wondering when he's going to call time, and then he shouts, "Crawl, Harry, crawl."

Jackie gets the ball and turns to throw, but when he sees Harry there in the base path moaning and rolling around, he holds it and starts trotting in to see what happened to Harry.

"CRAWL HARRY" Shellins is yelling at the kid, and Harry hears it, and he shakes his head no, he can't crawl, and this time Shellins bawls it out, "CRAWL."

Harry's eyes are clenched shut, and he doesn't even open them, but he straightens out on the base path and digs his fingernails in, and starts pulling himself towards home plate. He can't move his legs much but his toes are pushing him just a little.

Jackie finally wakes up and he loads and fires the ball in to the relay man, Webb.

Harry claws on, and he's about four feet from the plate.

Coach Shellins is still in his own dugout yelling "CRAWL." Our coach is yelling at Jackie, "THROW."

Webb takes the ball for the relay and turns and throws to Ned.

Harry digs in his fingernails for the last two feet and with a shove from his toes he reaches out and touches home plate with one finger just as Ned catches the ball and puts the tag on him.

"SAFE," calls the blue and they have their single run.

The second the blue calls him safe, both dugouts empty and both coaches go ripping over to Harry, and coach Shellins rolls him over and grabs his shoulders.

"What's wrong, what's wrong," he hollers, and Harry stops moaning and opens his eyes.

"My crotch! I'm gonna be sick."

Coach Shellins jerks Harry's belt open and unzips his pants and yanks them clear down to his knees. We all glance at the bleachers and there are a whole bunch of women and girls there and we crowd around Harry to shield him.

Coach Shellins signals one of his players to get the ice and our coach does the same and in an instant there's twenty pounds of crushed ice there.

Coach Shellins jerks down Harry's underwear, and shoves a towel under Harry and dumps all twenty pounds of ice right in. I mean, Harry's eyes aren't closed any more. They're so wide open I think they're going to pop right out of his head and the pupils are fixed and focused like he's staring at something eight miles straight up in the sky.

Coach pulls the towel up to hold the ice in place and then jerks the underwear up over that and then yanks Harry's pants up to cover the whole thing. He pulls Harry to his feet and we help lift him so he won't have to walk and we hold his pants up and crowd around so no one in the bleachers can see, and we all carry him back to his bench.

We all stand back a little while Coach Shellins waits to see what's going to happen. The only sound we get out of Harry is his teeth. They're beginning to chatter. Then he begins to shake all over from the cold.

I mean, what do you expect? Twenty pounds of cracked ice, right smack dab in the pants!

"Feel better Harry?", his Dad says, worried.

Harry's lips are moving but all we hear is his teeth chattering. He tries three times and can't say anything because he's shaking so hard and his teeth are clacking. He finally nods his head yes.

Coach Shellins looks at our coach and says, "Think I better take him to the doctor right now?"

Coach kneels down and presses around Harry's stomach a little and watches Harry's eyes while he's doing it. Harry's eyes still have that eight mile stare.

"I think he just pulled a muscle in his groin," our coach says. "I'd just watch him for a while and then take him on down to your doctor to be safe."

"I think you're right," Coach Shellins says.

He makes a substitution and the blue calls us back into play and we have to run back out to finish the game, which is one more inning.

During that inning, we keep glancing over at Harry.

He's shaking so bad the whole bench is trembling. The guys toss a couple of team jackets over his shoulders and pretty soon he's sitting there in the July heat, sweating, still shaking and his teeth are click-clacking.

Part way through the seventh inning, the ice is melting pretty bad and it starts to run down his legs. With one out to go, Harry is sitting in a great big puddle of water on the bench, and a lake of water around his feet. His pants are dripping wet and his shoes and socks are soaked. His teeth are still chattering from the ice, while he's sweating from the heat and the jackets. Both teams are turning their heads once in a while during the last of the seventh to keep anyone from seeing us laugh.

When the game ends, we all crowd around again while his Dad pulls off his pants and underwear, and wraps him in a couple of towels and we carry him to his Dad's car for a ride to the doctor's office to be sure nothing is seriously hurt.

We gather the equipment and coach calls us around.

"Listen up," he says, and we can feel the tension in his voice. "Tomorrow's our last practice before the final game of this half, and we play the Orioles. Neither one of us have been beaten this half."

We all silently look at each other while we wonder how we got down to the last game of the second half without a loss. Can we get past the Orioles? Our minds sort of reach out to touch the question, then back off like it's too thorny.

"Practice tomorrow at four o'clock", coach says.

We all show up a little early for the practice, and it goes okay, so-so. We go through all the motions, and there's the usual chatter, and me and Jackie spend some extra time with Mendoza, both batting and fielding.

But there's some unspoken, nagging little place in our brains that keeps us from being wide open, free, easy, and we don't know what it is. Like a hangnail you can't see, but won't go away.

15

BAD TROUBLE WITH THE GEEZER

BY FOUR THIRTY BOTH TEAMS are gathered at the field, and we're all talking too much, too loud, too nervous. The Geezer came home early to bring me to practice, and he's gone home to get Mom because she didn't want to watch warmups.

By game time the bleachers are jammed, and some families are sitting on blankets.

The blue calls us to the plate. We're home team, and they bat first. He pulls his mask down and yells "Play ball," and the game is under way.

I strike out the first two batters, and Randy throws the third one out on an easy grounder, and my arm feels good, and everything feels like it's working. We trot in and look at the batting order the coach has posted on the chain link, and I get a surprise. I am moved back from seventh batter to fifth batter, one of the cleanup spots. At .355, my batting average is second high on the team, right behind Bernie.

Ned connects on the third pitch with a clean, hard shot, right to their shortstop, and he's thrown out at first.

Randy hits a long, strong fly to left field, and their fielder makes a spectacular running, diving grab and hangs onto it. Second out.

Chin hits a bullet right down third base line and their third baseman dives and spears it, and we're down, one, two three, and we're going into the second, no score for either team.

Second inning, I put their next three batters down, one two three, and we trot in for our bats.

Bernie hits a towering shot out to center field and it's caught for the first out.

I hit a solid drive to their second baseman and I am thrown out at first base.

Denny strikes out and we are down, one two three.

I get a premonition and it sends a chill down my back.

By the bottom of the third, with the score zero to zero, I think we're going through one of those rare games where you knock the ball all over the field with great hits, but somehow, every one of them is straight at one of their players.

We finally get Jackie on base with a single, move him to third on another single, and the next ball is hit right to the second baseman who turns a double play to end the inning. Next inning we get Chin to first on a walk, advance him to second on a sacrifice bunt by Stone, move him to third on a sacrifice fly, and the next batter hits a dribbler right back to their pitcher and is thrown out. We're hitting the ball all over the place but no score.

By the bottom of the fifth inning, we're starting to believe there are little invisible elves out there, guiding our key hits into their gloves. It's crazy! I'm pitching a shutout. I mean, they haven't even come close to getting a hit. And our guys have hit solid sixteen times, and every time, it's been right at one of their players, or they've made some wild, circus catch. They've walked four of our guys, and with all the hits we should have had about ten guys across the plate by now and be winning ten to zip. But every break in the game has gone to them, and none to us. We know it and they know it, and they're out there white faced and silent, because they know we're beating the daylights out of them, only the score doesn't show it.

For us, it's becoming one of those games you have in your worst nightmares, when you try to run and can't, and you try to throw and your arm won't move.

Top of the sixth and the score is still zero to zero.

I start to remember the world series where the Yankees and the Pirates played it off in the 1950's or 1960's. Went a full seven games. The Pirates won, but in the seven games, they made about six runs, and the Yankees made about thirty. The problem was, the pirates won four games at one to zip, or two to one, and the Yankees won the other three games about ten to zip. After it was over, even the pirates said the Yankees were the best team. But that didn't change the fact the Pirates won the world series on four freak games.

And here we are, the same kind of thing happening to us. Just a freak. Won't happen again this century. We're beating these guys big time, but the score is tied.

I put them down in order in the top of the sixth, and we go to bat. Ned bats second. He steps in there, and their pitcher's showing the strain, and throws a wild pitch high and outside. Ned steps out of the box, then comes back in, and their pitcher takes the sign from the catcher, and winds up and lets go a fastball.

It's hard and wild, and way inside. Ned tries to jerk back, but he can't get far enough in time and the ball smacks the back of his left hand, on the bat. Ned drops the bat and grabs his hand, and doubles over. Coach shouts "Time" and Ned trots over to the ice bucket and shoves his hand in. In ten seconds we're all jammed around him, waiting.

Coach Briggs gently tugs each finger and watches Ned's eyes, and he's got them clenched shut and his teeth gritted.

"Bad pain?," he asks.

Ned shakes his head no. "Numb."

"Bend 'em."

Ned slowly clenches his fist and then opens it and Briggs starts to breathe again. "I don't think they're broke," he says.

Coach Stern rounds his lips and blows air. "Ned, keep that hand in ice. Bernie, you catch. Mendoza, right field."

We all look at the ground for a second while Mendoza swallows hard.

Coach takes a minute to settle us down. "Stay cool. They're getting the breaks but it can't last forever. You're playing good ball. Okay, let's go."

I look at their next three batters, and they're the meat of their lineup, numbers two, three and four. The best they've got.

The first one doesn't have much power but he has great hand-eye coordination and makes contact nearly every time. He's a hard man to strike out.

I move him back with a high fast ball, and then with a looping curve that looks like it's going to bean him before it drops away. Two balls, but when he comes back to the plate, he's tentative, not sure what to expect, but he knows I'm behind him, two balls, no strikes.

Then I bear down. A fastball over the outside edge, and a sinker that hits the dirt right behind the plate, and a slow curve that he chases, and he's out.

Their second batter has power, but those power hitters strike out a lot because they're swinging for the fence.

A sinker, then a fastball inside that moves him back, a curve that straightens him just before it slopes off away from him for a called strike, and then a fastball, six inches higher than he likes them, and he goes down with a monster swing that forces a grunt when he misses.

Two down, and I have thirteen strike outs.

Their heavy hitter cleanup man walks to the plate and I look him over and call up how he hits. He's a pull hitter, and he likes fastballs just below the belt level.

Bernie signs curve and I shake him off and he signs sinker and I shake him off, and then he signs fastball, and I nod yes, and I can see Bernie thinks I've lost my mind because this guy eats fastballs.

I deliver it low but still in the strike zone, and on the outside edge, and it catches him by surprise because he didn't expect a fastball first up. He's quick enough to get around on it but not quick enough to hit it solid, and he fouls it. Strike one.

Bernie signs curve, and I throw the perfect curve. It starts shoulder high inside, and then hooks at the last second down and away and crosses the plate, and this guy knows it's a strike and starts his swing, but he realizes he'll never hit it with any power at all, and he checks his swing, but too late, and I'm way ahead of him, two strikes, no balls.

I shake off the curve sign from Bernie and I wait for the sinker.

The guy starts to swing like it's a fastball, but then he realizes it's a sinker, and he can't check his swing, so he drops his bat and I can see the desperation on his face as he hopes he'll get enough of it to at least get it out of the infield. His swing is low and hits the ball on the bottom, and the ball arches out in a routine, garden variety, everyday pop out to short right field, and for an instant I feel relief. This is their last batter. With him out, we've got a shutout, and we can win if we get a run in the bottom of the inning.

And then it flashes in my mind.

Mendoza!

My heart stops.

I turn and watch it, holding my breath. The guy is rounding first base before Mendoza starts trying to line himself up to make the catch.

Jackie breaks from center field towards right field as hard as he can run to back up Mendoza.

If Mendoza had just stood there it would have hit him smack on his head. But he doesn't. He moves forward two steps and raises his mitt above his face. The ball thumps into the grass right behind him and he turns just as Jackie leans to make a bare handed pickup on the dead run and Mendoza slams into Jackie and they go down in a pile on top of the ball.

The guy rounds third and his coach is pumping him on to home plate and he crosses standing up.

A home run on an error.

I can't believe it. None of us can. We stand around for a second, scuffing our toes in the dirt and then we trot over to see if Jackie and Mendoza are all right, and they get untangled and Jackie picks the ball out of the grass. We don't know quite what to say and we all go back to our positions and I face the next batter.

Three pitches and he's out.

We have our bats in the bottom of the inning, and we still have a chance. We're silent while Randy picks up his bat and walks out to home plate.

They walk him.

Chin pops out, and Bernie comes up next and drills a single out past second baseman and now we got one man out, a runner on first and second. I'm up next.

They run me to a full count and then their pitcher makes a mistake and I get a walk.

The electricity starts. Bases are loaded, one out, and Denny comes to the plate.

Denny takes a called ball and a called strike and then whacks one that goes nearly straight up and straight down and is caught by their catcher just in front of the plate.

The crazy things are still happening! Denny never hit a pop fly like that before in his life.

Two out, bases full and I think about Ned coming up to bat next and I still have hope until I remember.

Mendoza! He's in for Ned.

We all watch as Mendoza picks up a bat and starts for the plate and we yell at him, "Come on, Mendoza, you can do it. Just meet it."

Mendoza breathes deep and squares and cocks the bat over his shoulder.

The first pitch is high and outside and Mendoza swings.

We groan, but no one says anything.

The next pitch is a curve and Mendoza watches it cross the plate, a strike.

"Watch for a fastball," I call to him, and he nods.

The next pitch is a fastball. Mendoza swings after it has hit the pitchers mitt, the blue bawls "Steerike" and jerks up his right hand. Mendoza's out and the game's over, and they win.

The Orioles bench goes crazy, and the bleachers are shouting, and our guys stand there still, watching while Mendoza drops his head and walks back to the bench dragging his bat.

"It's okay," I say to him when he passes, but he doesn't even look at me. He knows.

The final score is one to zip, their favor, but because their single run came on a fielding error by Mendoza, it is not scored as a hit. I just pitched a no hit ball game, and still lost!

We line up to exchange high fives with the Orioles, and we're not saying a word as we slap hands. We go back to our bench and plop down or stand around, and we stare at the ground, trying to figure out how we beat those guys into the ground and still lost. It's the weirdest feeling I've ever had following any ball game.

The Geezer and Mom come over, and Ming Chin and Claire Billman are behind them, and they're cheerful, and come on like so what, it was just a ball game.

The team just sits there like lumps, not wanting to say or do anything. Mendoza slumps at the far end of the bench, away from everybody, and I know his heart is broken.

Then this crazy thing happens. It starts with Jackie.

Jackie starts to shake with a silent chuckle. Stone looks at him like he's lost his mind, and Jackie laughs out loud. Stone starts to laugh because he thinks Jackie's flipped out, and then Denny picks it up, and Bernie busts out laughing that wild cackle of his, and Ned's sitting there with his hand packed in ice, and he laughs.

Randy grabs the hose over by the tree and turns it on full blast, and he comes charging in spraying everybody, and Bernie grabs him and Chin grabs the hose, and he soaks down everybody he can, and I grab it from Chin and soak him, and there we are, about four of us wrestling for the hose, and everybody's getting soaked, and we're getting muddy and drenched, and then everybody piles on.

I see Mendoza sitting down there all alone, not caring, wishing he was dead, and I give Bernie a sign, and he and Chin follow me and we grab Mendoza and jerk him into the free for all, and Bernie sits on him while I soak him down.

His mother yells and then she sees we're all laughing, and Mendoza starts to grin, and then he laughs, and I mean, this insanity goes on for five minutes before Stone turns off the hose.

We stand there grinning at each other, soaked, muddy, hats all over the place, hair a mess, and all of a sudden it hits me.

The team has come together!

Mendoza blew it big time and lost the championship game for the second half for us, and three weeks ago we'd have let him suffer. But he's right there with us now, soaked, muddy, shirttail out, hat gone, belly hanging over his belt, but he's one of us. He's still a fat, slow, rotten baseball player, but he's *our* fat, slow, rotten baseball player.

Coach looks at us and shakes his head. We're the sorriest looking team he ever saw, standing there messed up.

"Playoff is in two days at five o'clock. No practice tomorrow. Stay loose and relax."

We load up the gear and I get in the back seat and Geezer drives me and Mom home.

"Playoffs in two days?" he asks.

"Yeah," I say.

"Ten inning rule still applies."

Only then does it break dawn in my mind. I can only pitch three innings in the championship game, and suddenly I feel everything go out of me. Jackie can't hold the Orioles. We won't have a chance. It's a pretty quiet ride home after that.

I shower and lay on my bed until mom calls us for supper. I pick at my food and excuse myself before dessert and go up to my room. It's a long time later that the Geezer walks in.

"What you going to do about it," he asks.

I shrug. There's nothing I can do.

"Win it with the bat," he says.

Yeah, right. We hit the ball everywhere it could be hit today, and we lost. Jackie can't hold those guys. We came a long ways, but we're going to lose it all. I look at him disgusted, and I say nothing.

"Get on down in the garage now," Geezer says, "and go to work on the batting tee. Get back to fundamentals."

I just sit there silent.

"What's the matter? You given up all ready?"

I shake my head, but there's nothing to say.

"Come on," he says, "let's . . ."

Something inside me rises up. "No. We done all we could. Jackie can't do it."

"You don't know . ."

I suddenly stand and face him, my feet apart. "It's real easy for you. You don't have to go out there and do it. You just have to lecture me, and it's not fair."

I can hardly believe what I'm saying.

"You don't know what it feels like," I continue, my voice rising. "You don't know how it is to have you always there lecturing and telling me everything."

His face goes blank and his jaw drops for a minute. "Always lecturing? What you talking about?"

"Like right now. Get the batting tee. It don't matter if I get the batting tee."

He starts to say something, and then stops, and I've never seen him stumble around for words. "That's lecturing?"

"Yeah! And I don't ever do anything right! You always got something to say, something I should have done different. What's the use trying? I'll never satisfy you."

He stands there froze for a minute. "What are you talking about?"

"YOU! No matter what, you just keep telling me, do this, do that. You don't know how I feel. You don't care. All I get is another lecture, no matter what." I feel my voice starting to crack and there's a sudden rush inside and I choke down the feeling I'm going to cry.

His eyes drop and he stands there under the light for a long time, looking at the carpet.

"Joe," he finally says, real quiet, "I didn't know that's how you felt. You got to understand. People get old, and they forget. I forgot how it feels to be young, and to want something bad. I forgot how it feels to try so hard and see it all slipping away. I just forgot. It's my fault."

I can see the pain in his eyes, and a look like he's bewildered, and I've never seen him this way.

He continues. "I didn't mean to lecture. I just forgot how it was, and all I saw was what I figured should be done about it, and I guess I got lost. I guess I didn't know I was that old yet."

He shakes his head and I can see a sadness I've never seen before.

"I didn't mean to lecture. I meant to help. I . . I hope you can understand."

I see pleading in his eyes, and for the first time in my life, I see a little fear. I can hardly believe it. He's never been afraid of anything, ever!

He turns and walks out, and I'm left there standing in my room, absolutely shook that I would ever, ever talk to the Geezer like I did, and shocked at how it struck him.

16

ME AND DAD AND THE CHAMPIONSHIP GAME

SIX O'CLOCK IN THE MORNING
is dark and cool, and the neighborhood is dead quiet. The only
sound is my bat whacking a taped ball off the tee, into the big
block wall. At 6:30 the Geezer walks out the garage door and
looks at me, then goes back in.

Head down, look at the ball until you make contact, swing
level, follow through. By 6:45 I'm sweating. Seven o'clock I
hear the Geezer start the car to go to work and I walk around
to watch the car disappear at the curve. I wish he had said
something this morning. Anything. I'm so mixed up inside I
have to keep telling myself to concentrate. Head down, look,
swing level, follow through.

At 7:30 Mom makes German pancakes. I sprinkle cinnamon
sugar into the melted butter and roll them up tight.

"Cinnamon rolls?," I ask her.

She sighs. "How many?"

"Three dozen."

Eight o'clock I make the first call. "Two o'clock."

"Cinnamon rolls?," Bernie asks.

"Yeah."

I hang up and keep punching numbers.

By two o'clock we're all at the field.

I look at Ned's hand, wrapped heavy with stretch wrap. "What did the doctor say?"

"It aint busted. X-Rays were okay."

"How's it feel?"

"Okay. Sore."

"You play tomorrow?"

"Maybe," he says.

I turn to the other guys. "Let's start drills. Mendoza, come with me."

Bernie and Chin start infield and outfield routines while I take Mendoza under the big tree by the hose.

"Okay. You blew it big time because you forgot to watch the stupid ball until you hit it!"

He looks embarrassed while I tear into it.

"Now take the bat and I'm going to throw easy. I don't care what else you do but I'm going to kill you if you don't watch the ball. You got that?"

He nods and takes the bat and I back up ten steps and start lobbing them in.

Ten minutes later he's making contact with every ball.

"Okay, we're going to the plate and do it for real."

Bernie hunkers behind the plate while I throw to Mendoza, and ten minutes later Mendoza's making contact with one in three while I throw some stuff, not too hard.

"Okay, full out," I say, and I crank up a fastball.

He swings and misses, and I jump all over him. "You didn't watch the ball, idiot! Watch the stupid ball."

He concentrates, and pretty soon he's watching them all, clear to the bat. Then he hits one, and a minute later, another, and another.

I can see it in his eyes. He's starting to feel a teeny tiny little grain of confidence.

Fifteen minutes later I call to him and Bernie. "I'm getting a drink," and I head for the hose and they follow. We drink and run the hose over our heads, and go back to it.

Twenty minutes later Mendoza's standing there at the plate, hair plastered to his forehead by sweat, but he won't stop. I'm throwing some regular stuff, not too hard, and no curves or sinkers, but he's making contact with one out of three. That's batting .333, and in his life, he never dreamed he could do it. None of us did.

"Okay, we field. Bernie, hit."

Bernie grabs a bat and I march Mendoza out to the outfield, and Bernie whacks a high fly. Mendoza watches it rise, and he starts too late and doesn't get to it in time.

"Come on, you dummy, I told you a hundred times. You got to start when the ball leaves the bat."

He looks at me with tortured eyes. "I can't see it that quick."

"Yes you can," I insist. "Now watch."

Bernie cracks another one, and again Mendoza waits too long.

"Mendoza," I say, "I'll kill you if you aren't moving when the ball hits the bat! I don't care where you move, just move somewhere!"

Bernie hits another one, and Mendoza's moving as soon as the ball leaves the bat, exactly the wrong direction. He stops and turns too late, and then looks at me and his face is begging for mercy.

"Okay," I tell him. "You did okay. You moved. Do it again."

Twenty minutes later he's moving with the crack of the bat every time, and now he's moving the right direction more than half the time.

Fifteen minutes later he's moving the right direction most of the time. He's puffing, and his shirt is sweated, but the look in his eyes? In his whole life he's never looked like that. For the first time, he feels like he's not a fat, slow, dumb kid. He looks like he might do it right, just once.

"More water," I say, and the three of us gather at the hose. We drink and I soak my head for a minute and then jerk my hat back on and we call in the guys.

"Enough?," I ask while they share the hose. They're all sweated out, red faced.

They nod yes and I hear "Yeah" a few times.

I tear open the brown paper bag and we divide up three dozen cinnamon rolls while we sit in the shade of the tree and drink from the hose.

"That hand feel any better," I ask Ned.

"It don't feel no worse," he answers.

"Going to try it tomorrow?"

"Sure."

I think about it for a minute before I say it. "Mendoza, you ready." All eyes turn to him for a split second.

Mendoza looks at me and his eyes are steady and his head is up. He's not looking at the ground any more, like a born loser.

He shrugs. "I'm not very good."

I pause with my cinnamon roll. "I didn't ask that. You ready to give it a real try?"

"Yeah," he says firmly, "I am."

I start chewing again. "Okay. You don't, we kill you with a bat."

He grins and Stone grins, and Denny Stott says, "Right there in front of the bleachers."

We finish and I wad up the torn brown bag while Stone turns off the hose, and we leave. I pedal part way with Mendoza, and then I watch him while he continues on to the gravel pit, with my old mitt safely draped on the handlebar of that weird bicycle with the tricycle seat and no fenders.

On the day of a season championship game, you live in a new world. You get up in the morning and breakfast tastes like cardboard. You snap at people on the phone, and you can't sit in one place more than two minutes, and if the dog barks, your mind invents ways to murder him.

When the Geezer leaves for work, I hear him tell Mom he'll be home for the game, but he doesn't say a word to me. He hasn't said anything since I ripped into him two nights ago. I want so bad to tell him I didn't mean all that, that I'm sorry, but I don't know how to do it, and he's not making it any easier.

Mom says she'll drive me to the field for the game, but I tell her I'd rather use the bicycle, and she can come with the Geezer when he gets home.

Griffith Park is big. It has two complete baseball diamonds, and a soccer field, and half a dozen asphalt basketball courts, some tennis courts, and rest rooms, and a picnic area with a lot of tables, and a hundred oak tress and spruce trees. At the north baseball diamond, due east of home plate exactly one hundred ten measured yards, right out behind where the left fielder usually takes his position, is a big, beautiful oak. Twenty yards past it is a rose bed, and past that is a broad cement walk that leads to the rest rooms. I've noticed that oak a dozen times, but never like I would notice it later today.

I get there thirty minutes early, and when Mendoza shows I pull him aside and shove a bat in his hands.

"Show me."

He takes his stance and drops his head forward and makes a smooth, even stroke while his eye follows the flight of an imaginary baseball.

"Okay. You're in the field and the batter gets a hit. What do you do?"

"I move."

"Where."

"To the ball."

"Good. If you forget, what happens?"

"You guys kill me with a bat."

"Where?"

"In front of the bleachers."

He grins while I hold a sober face. "Do you believe it."

"Yeah."

"You got it right."

Then crazy things start to happen. A big TV van pulls in and guys start stringing out fat cables and setting up a big three legged TV camera behind the backstop. Mayor Carlyle shows up and starts shaking hands with everybody and smiling all over the TV guys. People pull into the parking lot and spread blankets on the grass, and they got kids and big thermos jugs filled with ice and lemonade.

The aircraft carrier pulls in, and Ming Chin gets out, and her husband with her. Then that big white Cadillac pulls in, and Claire Billman gets out, and on the other side, Dr. Billman gets out, and I nearly flop over in a dead faint! We hear the Mendoza truck for five minutes before it turns into the parking lot and clatters to a stop, and Mendoza trots over to help his Mom and Dad unload the army. Three blankets and two big thermos jugs, and two bags of diapers, and the kids are all scrubbed and wearing their white shirts and blouses and black pants.

I'm watching, and finally the Geezer and Mom arrive. They

find the Billmans and the Chins, and Rosa and Papa Mendoza leave the older kids to tend the younger ones, and they come sit with the other team parents in one place in the bleachers, and they're talking and gabbing like they've known each other forever.

The Oriole parents are doing the same thing, and people we've never seen before just keep pouring in. A newspaper reporter corners both coaches and pumps them for all kinds of information, and they're calling it a grudge game, the game of the year, the game of the titans, - all that nutty stuff newspapers say.

We run through warmups, and give the field to the Orioles, and we watch them warm up, and one thing we see. The only thing they care about in this whole world, is proving it wasn't a fluke when they beat us two days ago. I'm standing there leaned against the chain link watching them, when I hear the Geezer behind me, and I turn to face him, and I'm ready for the usual lecture about how to bat and how to play this game.

He looks at me and I can see he's trying to find words. He finally says, "I've taken some time to think over what you said."

I cut him off. "I didn't mean it. I don't know what happened. I just . ."

That's as far as I can go.

"Joe," he says, "don't worry about it. You go play your own game. Whatever you do, it'll be right. Go get 'em."

I want to say more, but before I can start, he gives me a thumbs up, and turns back and climbs back up by Mom.

I stand there like I been hit by lightning. In my life, I never expected to hear him say that. Something turns over inside me, and it's like magic! Suddenly, unexpectedly, I understand! It's like every thought I ever had about him goes up in the air and comes down different than before. All the lectures, all the orders - I didn't understand! He wasn't lecturing. He was doing all he could to teach me. It was me, not him, that was wrong. How could I miss it? How could I have been so dumb? I look at him again, and I'm seeing someone I've never seen before!

The Orioles finish warmups and trot back to their bench, and coach calls us together for just a minute. "No strategy, no gimmicks. We grind it out one inning at a time. There's a change in the batting order. We got two cleanup batters. Bernie bats fourth, Joe bats ninth, so we can get anybody home who gets on. Gives us a one two punch. Joe, you start on the mound for the first inning, and the sixth and seventh. Ned, how's the hand?"

Ned holds it up and it's still wrapped.

Coach asks, "Can you play?"

Coach Briggs answers. "Doctor says he can play with it, at least for a while unless it starts to hurt too much."

Coach pauses for a minute. "Okay, Ned you start behind the plate."

Then Coach glances at the blue, who's waving at us. "Let's go. Stay loose and easy."

And right there, Chin makes the move that pulls it all together. He steps forward and thrusts out his hand, and looks at us. His face is still like a stone Buddha, but those eyes! They're saying, loud and clear, "We're a team."

Denny catches the idea first, and he slaps his hand down on top of Chin's and holds on, and then Jackie, and then we all do, and we're standing there in the circle with white and black and yellow and brown hands piled up, and right then, at that moment, we're not different colors any more, and we're not rich or poor, or good or bad ball players. We're a team.

"Hey," the blue calls, "you want to forfeit this game?"

We break and trot over.

In a championship game, home team is decided by a flip of a coin. The blue calls both catchers and tells Ned to call it and Ned calls heads and it lands heads.

They bat first.

Ned pulls his mask down and gingerly slips his sore hand inside his mitt while I walk around the mound rubbing the ball, and the team goes to their places. Ned nods to the blue and the blue bawls "Play ball" and their first batter picks up an aluminum bat and walks out to the plate.

It's starting. The championship game. That odd, calm feeling begins its work, and I settle down. I look at the batter's eyes, and study him while I call up his strengths and his weaknesses.

Ned signs curve and I shake it off, and he signs fastball, and I give him that slight head nod. This first pitch has got to be a statement. It has to say, forget all the hype, we're coming straight at you.

I deliver and the batter swings and the ball whacks into Ned's glove before his bat reaches the plate. I see Ned flinch a little, despite the fact he's got a leather half sole inside his mitt.

There's a murmur in the bleachers, and one loud, clear, truck driver voice louder then the others.

"IN YOUR FACE!." Then laughter breaks out all over the place. It's Mom. Heaven only knows where she got that one. Somewhere she's been expanding her grasp of baseball.

Ned signs curve, I shake him off, he signs fastball, and I deliver, and the guy swings again, late.

"Steeeerike two," calls the blue and the batter knows he's dead.

Ned signs curve and I take it and deliver, and the ball slopes in from right to left, dropping all the way, and the batter knows he couldn't hit it with a tennis racket, but it's a strike so he has to try, and he misses it a foot.

Three pitches, three strikes.

The second batter comes up and Ned signs sinker. The batter is looking for a fastball and he swings and misses.

Ned signs curve, and I deliver, and the ball starts out head high and inside, and the batter leans back like he's going to be hit, and then it drops off to the left and picks up the inside corner of the plate for a called strike. I got this guy down bad with two called strikes.

The next one is a fast ball, six inches above his belt and he sees it coming but he can't get around on it in time and goes down for out two, swinging.

Six pitches, two strikeouts.

Ned throws the ball back and I rub it for a minute and I signal Ned and he tells the blue we need time out. I give the coach a head sign and he comes out.

"Coach, what do you think about walking their next two guys and then I take out their number five batter, like the last time. Give Jackie the bottom of their batting order for second inning?"

Coach takes off his hat and scratches his head a minute and then puts it back on.

"Chancy. Can you handle it?"

"Yeah."

"Go for it."

I throw eight straight balls and walk their next two men, and right in the middle of it comes this foghorn voice again.

"YOU BLIND OR SOMETHING?"

The usual uproar breaks out while mom smiles. I hear the Geezer say something to her and then there's more laughter and I shut it out of my mind while I study their next batter.

This guy is a pretty good hitter but he's radical. Once in a while he blasts one a hundred yards, and you never know where it's going. He strikes out a lot, pops out some, and gets singles.

Ned signs sinker and I deliver and he tries to correct and gets enough of it to tip it foul, and it whacks into Ned's chest protector.

Ned signals sinker again and I deliver and the batter swings and misses.

Ned signs fastball and this guy thinks it is a third sinker and it streaks over his bat for a third strike.

Top of the first inning is over. They didn't score, and the best batters in their order are gone for Jackie in the second.

I trot to the bench and the mood is controlled eagerness.

Their pitcher warms up and the blue calls for a batter, and Ned goes out, our first batter of the game.

He lays down a single over second base and gets to first safely.

Randy lays a perfect bunt right down third base line and beats it out to first base, Ned goes to second.

Chin pops out to the second baseman.

One out, men on first and second.

Bernie comes up and whacks a double right over third baseman's head, out into left field and Ned and Randy both score.

Denny comes up and lines out a single past short stop and Bernie scores, with Denny holding on first.

One man out, one man on first, three runs scored.

Webb hits a pop fly and the first baseman runs back and loses it in the sun and then picks it up again and then loses it again and he drops it in fair territory. Webb is on first base and Denny is on second.

Webb gets hit by a bad pitch and goes to first base and we got bases loaded, one down.

Stone hits an infield pop up and is out on the infield fly rule.

Two down, bases loaded. I take the bat and go to the plate.

I take a called ball and a called strike, and then I settle in and the next pitch is a fastball and I connect and it clears third base and drops in the outfield fair, and rolls foul. I pull up on second, but all the runners have scored.

Two down, six runs, and I'm on base.

We're back at the top of our order, and Ned hits a grounder right back to the pitcher and is thrown out.

We batted ten men, got six runs, left one man on.

Top of the second inning, I catch Jackie before he trots out to the mound.

"Don't sweat it if they get a run. Just give it your best."

Their first batter, sixth man in their lineup, isn't too strong, and Jackie runs it to a full count with him before the guy cracks out a single and is on first.

Second batter hits a blooper and Randy spins and sprints but can't get there, and it drops fair, and they got a man on first and second, no outs.

Their next man takes two called balls and then Jackie gets a little nervous and accidentally brushes the guys arm with the next pitch and the guy's on base free.

Bases loaded, no one out.

Their next batter is last on their batting order, and by far their weakest hitter. So what does he do? He swings blind at the first pitch and drives a double out over Webb and clears the bases.

They got three runs, a man on second, and no one out.

I take a deep breath. No one is getting anything for free in this game, and it's going to be a high scorer if this keeps up.

Next batter is their lead off batter at the top of their order, and he gets a single. Their runner advances to third.

Next batter makes contact but it goes right to Webb on second base and he underhands to Randy who tags second base and relays to first for a double play, but the runner on third scores.

Bases are empty and they got four runs and there are two out.

Jackie bears down and gets their next batter to hit a high, towering fly ball to Bernie and he catches it for the third out.

Going into the bottom of the second, we still hold the edge, six to four. We go down, one two three. Just bam bam bam. After that big first inning, who can explain it?

Top of the third they go down, one two three. Jackie isn't doing anything different. He's giving it all he's got, but he did that in the second inning. One of those crazy things.

Bottom of the third, we got two men out and two men on when I get back at the bat and I get a single and drive in one more run. Ned grounds out next, and that is our third out.

The score is seven to four, our favor.

Top of the fourth, they get two men on base with one out and we're ready to try for a double play but Randy commits the first error of the game and underthrows Webb on second and the ball rolls out into right field. Both base runners score and they got a man on first and one out. Score is seven to six on the error.

Their next man pops out. Two down, a man still on first.

Their next batter hits a high fly ball into foul territory right in front of our bench and Ned gets over to it and makes the catch for the third out.

Score, seven to six going into the bottom of the fourth.

We load the bases with no one out and Denny hits a line drive right to their third baseman. He snags it, touches his bag and makes a hard throw to second and catches Chin half a step short of getting back to the bag.

A triple play. Inning is over.

Top of the fifth, we are still ahead one run, seven to six.

Then the whole world turns around.

Jackie has given all he had in the three innings he's pitched. He is still pitching strong, but he just hasn't got quite enough tools to make it last through the next inning. When we go back out to the field, I give a head signal and we gather round the mound.

"Just give it what you got, and it'll be good enough."

He nods and we all whack him on the back like guys do and trot out to our positions.

They get two on base, first and second, and then Jackie strikes out their next batter.

Their next hitter cracks out a single and loads the bases.

One man out, bases full.

Their next man steps up and I feel a rise in my stomach. He's their cleanup man. He is a solid, strong hitter. I feel a little fear for Jackie.

Jackie blows a strike past him and then two balls and he knows he's been lucky so far. Ned gives him the curve signal and I can read it clear from right field where I'm playing, and Jackie winds up and delivers.

The curve is too gentle.

The guy lays into it and I know from the "Tank" sound of the bat it's gone. It clears Denny's head and drops behind him in left field. Denny turns and runs while the base runners are pounding for home base.

It is a grand slam home run. All four runners score and suddenly they are ahead, ten to seven.

One stroke of a bat and the whole world is turned around.

I watch Jackie's shoulders sag and I signal to Ned and he calls time. I trot to the mound and the infield gathers.

"Hey, you got one more man. Get him. You're doing okay."

Randy says, "Yeah, get this next guy."

Jackie takes heart and runs the next batter to a full count and then throws this super slow, sweeping curve and the guy about dislocates his elbows trying to check his swing but he's too late. Called strike and they're through with the top of the fifth.

Score, ten to seven, their favor.

We add one run to ours in the bottom of the fifth, and it ends ten to eight, they're on top.

Top of the sixth. I take the mound and Jackie goes back to center field.

For just a second I hear the TV crew over there going crazy with their broadcast. "High scoring . . great hitting . . pitching duel . . tense . . unpredictable . ." it goes on and on with all the hype.

Yeah, it's a good ball game, but it isn't the game those guys are announcing. It's a gutty, sweaty, down in the trenches, give and take war.

"Batter up," the blue calls and I square off with their first batter.

Three pitches later he walks back to his bench, struck out looking.

Second batter, I get ahead of him, two strikes and one ball and he swings blind at the next pitch and hits a dribbler right back to me and I throw him out at first.

Two down.

Third man comes up and Ned signs fastball. I wind up and deliver and the guy doesn't even get the bat off his shoulder.

"Steerike," the ump calls and jabs his right arm out.

But it's not the strike I notice. It's Ned. When that one smacked into his mitt, he winced bad and jerked his hand back a little.

He signs curve, and I deliver, and the guy tries to check a swing but he's gone too far and it's strike two.

And again, I see Ned wince and shake his hand.

Ned signs another fastball inside to move the guy back, and I deliver hard and inside and the guy jumps back, but that's when it happens.

Ned catches it, but this time he cringes, and slowly tugs the mitt off his bandaged hand. I signal time and run to the plate while the coaches come trotting out. Coach unwinds the bandage and the hand is red and puffy. Briggs takes hold of it and puts a little pressure on it, and Ned pulls it back, and Briggs shakes his head.

Coach pats Ned on the shoulder. "We can't risk it. You did great." He turns to Bernie. "You catch. Mendoza, to right field."

We make the adjustments and no one says a word about Mendoza.

Bernie drops into his grasshopper crouch and signs fastball and I blow it past this batter for strike three, and they're finished in the sixth.

We take our turn at bat in the bottom of the sixth with two runs to make up, and we have just two more at-bats to do it.

Why does it always come down to the last inning or two, and one or two runs?

Webb gets a single and is on first.

Randy gets a single and we got men on first and second, no one out.

Chin hits sharply to their shortstop, who throws to third and that guy hits second in time to pull a perfect picture double play.

Two out, a man on first.

Bernie hits a towering pop fly to center and they catch it and we are finished with the sixth inning.

Seventh inning with them ahead, ten to eight.

We get our mitts from our bench, and I stop by Mendoza. "What do you do when they hit the ball?"

"Move."

"Do it, buddy."

Bernie whacks him on the back, and Chin trots out with him and stops at first while Mendoza goes on out to his place in right field.

I move their first batter back with a looping curve that he jerks away from.

Then I deliver a sinker and two fastballs and he's out on strikes.

Second batter comes up.

I put a fastball past him and it sobers him when he hears "Steerike" from the blue.

Second pitch is a slow curve and he pulls his swing to make contact and hits an easy bouncer right out to first base. Chin fields it and I cover first and we have our second out.

Third man comes to the plate. This guy is their erratic hitter. You can never tell what he's going to swing at, or where he's going to hit it. He swings at balls as often as he swings at strikes, and the ones he does hit he sprays all over the ball park. Long balls, bloopers, pop flys, dribblers, just anything. This kind of a hitter is a pitcher's nightmare.

I move him back with a fast ball, high and inside.

He steps back up to the plate like he didn't even notice.

This time I throw a curve and I take a big chance. I throw it right at his head, putting enough stuff on it to hook it back down towards the plate so it doesn't hit him. I will never hit a batter on purpose.

It looks like it is going to take his head off for a minute and then it peaks and starts its drop and comes back just like I planned it and is a called ball, low and inside.

It doesn't phase this guy. He's nuts.

I can't waste any more pitches.

I blow a fast ball past him for a called strike.

All he does is grind his cleats in deeper for the next pitch.

I look at Bernie and he sort of shrugs and then he gives me the three finger sign.

I deliver the sinker and this guy closes both eyes and swings with every pound he's got.

I hear the "tank" sound and I know he got a lot of it, but I watch it rise and realize it's a real high pop fly, headed for shallow right field.

Mendoza!

I swear you can hear the bees in the flowers and the seagulls in the air while every eye in the park is on that white ball, rising in a monster, curving arc out to right field, and I don't think anyone on our team is breathing.

I see Mendoza start to move back at the sound of the bat, but then he stops and studies the ball for a second or two, until he sees it's going to be high, but shallow. Then he starts forward.

I watch him and the ball at the same time, trying to judge whether they're going to meet before the ball hits the ground, and as it falls, it's clear Mendoza won't get there in time.

Then Mendoza turns it up a notch. I've never seen him move this fast in the whole season. His face is a study in concentration while his stumpy legs are pumping to push two hundred twenty pounds forward faster than he's ever moved in his life.

The ball is coming down like a bullet, and when it's thirty feet off the groundl, Mendoza starts to lean, and then he dives! This short, fat little guy dives!

Two hundred and twenty pounds hit the ground on one round belly and he rocks forward with his mitt shoved out as far as his arm will go, and the ball smacks into the webbing of his glove.

But he doesn't close the glove! The ball bounces right back out, two feet straight up, and comes right back down, and one more time, Mendoza stretches. The ball settles into the leather and he clamps it shut and he's made a snowcone catch.

For a second he just lays there on his belly, stretched out further than he's ever stretched in his life, and he can't believe he caught it.

Nine baseball hats and mitts sail into the air and we are shouting like we're crazy and the bleachers are going insane and we don't even call time. The whole team sprints over to right field and we grab him and we jerk him to his feet and pound him on the back and his behind, and we're yelling and I swear I never saw a look in my life like was on his face, like he had just proved to the world he could do it right. It made me want to cry.

Even the blues are clapping. We look at the bleachers, and there's Mendoza's army, twelve kids, hanging onto the chain link, shouting. Rosa's jumping up and down beside Mom and Claire, pumping her arms, shouting "SI SI SI," and Mr. Mendoza's got both hands in the air, waiving, shouting "VIVA VIVA VIVA." I don't know who Viva is, but who cares?

Even the parents of the Oriole team are applauding.

And I can't believe my eyes! There's the Geezer, on his feet, punching holes in the sky with his fists, yelling his head off, and right beside him, Mr. Billman's going through Olympic class gymnastics! I mean, there's this tall, dignified African American, dressed in a spotless, starched white shirt with gold cuff links and a deep blue tie and gold tie pin, and he's acting like an idiot! And next to him is this runty little Mr. Chin, doing a jig.

The blue yells "Play ball," but he just as well have saved his breath. It's five minutes before we gather up our hats and mitts and head for our bench. It takes us another couple minutes for us to sober up and look at where we are in this game.

We're in the bottom of the seventh, score still ten to eight, and either we make up two runs to tie, or three runs to win, or it's all over.

The bleachers and the TV guys settle down and the tension starts to build.

Our first batter is Denny. He lays down a solid single between third and short stop and is safe on first base.

Jackie pops out to the second baseman.

One down, Denny on first base.

Stone runs it to a full count, and their pitcher puts one right down the middle and Stone misses it and is out.

Two down, Denny still on first base. We're still alive, but barely, and I glance to see who's our next man at bat, and I catch my breath.

Mendoza!

Our bench goes silent for a split second while Mendoza walks to where the bats are hung in the chain link, and he finds the lightest one. Before he gets it out of the fence, I lean forward and catch his eye, and I slowly turn my head and eyes like I'm tracking a ball, and he understands.

Watch the ball.

"Come on, Mendoza," Bernie hollers. "You can do it."

"Just meet it," Ned yells.

And then the whole team is on their feet yelling for him while he walks to the batters box. He sets his feet and works his plant foot a little, and draws the bat back, ready.

Our bench quiets, and the Bleachers are like a tomb.

Relief floods over their pitcher when he sees Mendoza walk out. A fat little guy who hasn't got a hit in a ball game since he was born.

Their pitcher takes the sign and puts a slow, easy one right down the middle, and I understand what he's doing. He's making fun of Mendoza. Mendoza watches it come past and backs up a little and hitches up his pants and steps back into the batters box.

Their pitcher takes the second sign, winds up and delivers and Mendoza is watching it all the way, and it's a called strike two. He steps back and wrinkles up his nose and looks at his bat for a minute and steps into the box.

The pitcher's nearly smirking when he delivers the third pitch, and I know when it leaves his hand that it will be a ball outside. The pitcher hopes Mendoza will panic and try for it, and I hold my breath.

Mendoza locks onto it and watches it all the way in, and he

lets it go by.

"Ball," calls the blue.

The smirk disappers from the pitchers face and I watch as his mouth becomes a straight line. He takes the sign and I can see it in his eyes. He's through messing around with this fat nobody.

He winds up and I know before he delivers that it's going to be a fastball.

Mendoza watches it leave his hand and he starts his swing and he tracks it all the way while he swings, and he watches it hit his bat.

"Tink!" He hit it late and he hit it on the very end of the bat, and it's a really lousy little blooper, a little chip shot, but it's enough to arch out thirty feet past the first baseman and drop just inside fair territory before it rolls foul. The blue shoots his arm out and points fair and Mendoza has a hit!

For a split second he stands there in disbelief, and our team is shocked so bad we're froze like statutes, and then it's like a dam burst.

"RUN MENDOZA RUN." We're all standing behind the chain link jumping up and down, and the coaches are both in the box shouting, and the bleachers are in an uproar.

Their first baseman pivots and runs for the ball while Mendoza starts for first base. Denny is rounding second when Mendoza works up to a fast trot. Their pitcher stands there like he doesn't believe what's happened, while their first baseman chases the ball into the grass in foul territory, and Mendoza gets all two hundred twenty pounds wound up to what will pass for running. Even an average baserunner would make second base on this one, but Mendoza?

Their pitcher watches the first baseman barehand the ball out of the grass and turn to throw before he remembers that he has to cover first, and he starts for first at a run. We're watching and it's going to be close as to who gets to the base first, Mendoza or their pitcher.

The pitcher is running as hard as he can, and Mendoza is gaining a little speed and suddenly we know they're going to hit the base at the same time.

Their first baseman makes the underhanded toss to their

pitcher, and his lead foot is coming down just as Mendoza hits the bag and they collide, hard.

Two hundred and twenty pounds beats one hundred fifty pounds every time, in a collision. Their pitcher bounces off Mendoza like a golf ball off a Sherman tank and winds up ten feet from the base in a heap. The ball rolls out into the grass, and he sits up like he can't figure out where the ground went.

Denny hesitates on third, and the coach holds him, and Mendoza stands on first for a minute, and then he does this remarkable, crazy thing.

Mendoza sits down on first base! And I know why. He's never been there before in a game. He just wants to savor that moment for a minute or two.

The bleachers are going crazy. Rosa and twelve little Mendoza's are shouting but we can't hear them in the storm of sound, and all of us on the team are pounding each other on the back and shouting at him, "Beautiful beautiful beautiful."

The blue calls it all back to order and tells us to play ball, and it is only then that it hits me.

I'm clean up batter. I'm next.

I sober up and take stock. Bottom of the seventh, two out, two runs behind, our guys on the corners, first and third.

And then this thing happens. It's like it comes from somewhere deep inside and flashes in my brain. I'm seeing the Geezer when I was little, out there with me and a batting tee. Head down, watch, swing level, let your arms do it, follow through. Hit it right and you'll feel it clear to your knees. And later, when I'm in little league, my coach. Same message. Fundamentals. And this season. Listen to me, I'll raise your batting average 100 points. And after the last game. Win it with the bat. Get busy with the batting tee. He was there all the time. He never gave up, even when I started calling him The Geezer, and when I got smarty with him.

I turn to look at him, like he's going to give me another lecture, and I find him in the bleachers.

But there's no lecture. He looks at me and he gives me a sold thumbs up and it's like I can hear him. Play your own game. Whatever you do, you'll do it right. Go get 'em, Joe.

It all comes together for me. I turn to face their pitcher, and I block out the sound, and the tension, and I can see only one thing. The pitcher and the ball.

He takes his sign and he winds up, and his hand comes straight over and I read fastball the instant it leaves his fingers.

It seems like the next half second goes in slow motion. The ball comes in a straight line. I can see the rotation and I can see the seams. I start my swing when it's six feet out of his hand. I keep my head down and take my stride and my left arm stiffens and pulls and my right arm comes to full extension and stiffens, and I watch the ball come to the bat.

TUNK. I catch it dead center on the sweet part of the bat, just as my wrists start their rotation, and I got every pound onto it, and I feel it clear across my shoulders, down past my hips, clear to my knees, and in that instant I see the Geezer talking to me. Hit it right, you'll feel it clear to your knees. Sweet sweet sweet.

I take one look at the ball. It's headed straight towards the left fielder, and it's rising. I drop the bat and take my first step towards first base and with it, I shout at the top of my lungs.

"RUN MENDOZA".

Denny is half way to home plate while Mendoza is taking his first step towards second base.

From somewhere behind me the team is screaming, "RUN MENDOZA RUN."

I track the ball and I see their left fielder coming in on it, which means he thinks it will fall in front of him.

"RUN," I shout again at Mendoza, and he's working up to a heavy trot near second base when I round first. Denny's already on home plate, shouting at Mendoza with the rest of the team.

The bleachers have gone ballistic. The Mendoza's are jumping around shouting, clapping their hands, and Mom and Ming and Claire are grabbing each other and shouting, and the Geezer and Mr. Billman and Mr. Chin, and Papa Mendoza are going crazy.

I'm one step past first base when I see their left fielder stop dead in his tracks, and then start to back peddle, and then he turns and runs. The ball is still climbing when it clears his head by fifty feet, and it's headed straight for that big oak tree out there one hundred ten yards!

Mendoza is chugging towards third when I catch him, and when he's ten feet from third base I'm three feet behind him, shouting RUN RUN, and I can see sweat running down the sides of his cheeks, and I can hear him grunt as he gives it all he's got.

Mendoza labors into third base with everyone on the team yelling "run", and starts for home, and just before I round third I look one last time at the fielder and the ball. I see the ball rip through that oak tree, and a bushel of leaves and sticks fall out of it, and the ball rockets right on to the rose bed twenty yards further out and smacks into the rose bushes, three hundred ninety feet from home plate. The fielder is sprinting for the rose bed as hard as he can run. I round third and turn towards home, and now I'm nearly on top of Mendoza, matching him stride for slow stride, and we look for all the world like a Mutt and Jeff comedy dance team as we chug on towards home.

Their fielder gets to the rose bed and looks for a second before he jumps right into the middle of them and grabs the ball, and jumps back out. His socks are shredded by the thorns, and he's got scratches all over his arm and legs, but he clears the bushes and takes his two running steps and fires the ball to the cutoff man with everything that's in him.

Without Mendoza in front of me, I'd have crossed home plate before he ever got to the rose bed, but I can't pass Mendoza because under the rules I would be called out. I have to stay behind him.

The ball comes singing in to their shortstop while me and Mendoza are ten feet from home plate, and he turns and cocks and fires to the catcher when Mendoza's four feet from the base, and Griffith Park is in pandemonium.

With the ball in the air, Mendoza dives for home plate, head first, and I dive right on top of him. His outstretched hand slaps the rubber slab and mine slaps it right beside his, and the ball whacks into the pitchers mitt and he puts the tag on my back.

The blue has stepped to one side to get the best view he can of what he sees coming, and he sees it just the way it happened.

Mendoza, me, the ball, one two three.

He throws his hands out, palms down, and he shouts "YER SAFE," and there's no way anybody is going to hold the crowd.

An avalanche of sound drowns out everything in the park. I'm laying there on top of Mendoza for just a second, and then our team reaches us, and they jerk us onto our feet, and Bernie grabs Mendoza and hugs him clear off the ground. Chin and Jackie are all over me, and the rest of the team starts to pound on both of us. The TV guy is back there grinding away with his camera.

Then the crowd from the bleachers reaches us. Mom and Ming and Claire and Rosa are hugging everybody, and Mr. Billman and Mr. Chin and Papa Mendoza are grabbing anybody they can, and I work my way over to Mendoza, and I grab that fat kid and I hug him like a brother, and he hugs me back.

"You done it," I shout in his face. "You done it."

Suddenly I remember, and in the middle of this giddy chaos I turn and look, and there's the Geezer, working his way to me. I stand there, waiting, not knowing what to expect.

He throws both arms around me and he hugs me, and he pushes me back for a second and then he wraps me in those big arms and hugs me again.

"Beautiful! That's the best baseball I ever saw. Man, did you ever do it right."

In my life, I never hope to have a feeling like that again. I throw both my arms around him and he pounds me on the back, and I pound him, and then I back off and we're standing there grinning at each other like a couple of kids.

"Did you see it, Dad? Did you see that hit?"

"Did I see it? That was a big league home run. Man, that thing was still climbing when it hit that oak tree. If that tree hadn't been there, that thing would of reached the street."

The TV guy muscles in with his portable camera.

"You're Joe Russell," he asks.

"Yeah."

"I need a shot of you."

I look at him, and I look at my Dad. My dad. Not The Geezer. My Dad, who had been there always, watching, studying, giving me his time and everything he knew, but mostly, forgiving me for how I had abused him. I straighten my uniform and dust off my hat and set it square on my head, and I look Dad in the eye.

"Okay. You got it. Me and my Dad."

He drops his arm over my shoulder, and I drape mine over his, and he swallows hard, and I can feel my eyes are shiny, and we turn to face the camera together, grinning like a couple of big kids, me and Dad.